Aly held Shaylee's hand for courage when it was their turn to crawl up onto the table and slip down through the hole. It required some undignified wiggling to get through the hole, but soon they all stood in a small, mysterious wooded clearing.

"Where's the hole?" Rachel yelped. It had vanished after the last girl was through.

"There isn't enough magic to hold it open on this side," Eidermoss said. "And now that you've left your world, there isn't enough magic to hold it open there, either."

"You mean we're stuck here?" Shaylee wailed.

"Oh, no, Princess. Once you find the Wellspring and release the magic, you can open the hole in this world, or the door in your world, again."

"So we can only get home again if we succeed?" Rissa asked.

Eidermoss opened her eyes very wide. "Yes, I think so."

Creative
Girls Club ®

Adventure Book

Wellspring of Magic™

By Jan Fields

Cover and Illustrations by Ryan Durney

Annie's Attic ®

ISBN: 978-1-59635-147-9
Library of Congress Number: 2007931979

Published by DRG.
Creative Girls Club® is a registered trademark of DRG Texas, LP.

Printed in the USA
First printing, 2007

1 2 3 4 5 6 7 8 9

For my daughter Rachel,
whose imagination is filled with magic.

Alysa Cohen

Hello. My name is Alysa, but everyone calls me Aly. I have an identical twin sister, Rachel. It's funny to think of Rachel as my identical twin because we don't have much in common. She's always racing to do something, while I like to take my time and think things through. I tell Rachel that she uses so many more bandages than I do because she's always in a rush. I love plants and painting because plants and paintings rarely move, while she prefers animals because they're always on the move, just like her. I spend a lot of time painting plants—you should see the mural I just started painting on my bedroom wall. It's going to be a painting of the most fantastic, magical garden you've ever seen!

I like the idea of gardens being magic. Mom and I are going to plant a garden in our backyard, and I want to make it the kind of garden where you can imagine fairies hiding in the flowers. Wouldn't that be beautiful? I know I'm probably going to have to do a lot of the work in the garden, but I don't mind. My mom says she's planning to be home more now that we've moved out of the city, but I'm not holding my breath. She loves being a lawyer and I figure she'll be back to a crazy schedule before long.

My dad is a teacher and a great one at that. It didn't take long for him to snag a job at the high school here. So we're already getting settled in.

Rachel and I have met all the girls in the neighborhood, and we like them a lot. We get together in this little old building in the middle of the park that's at the center of our neighborhood. The park is very overgrown and totally magical looking with lots of ivy-covered statues. Dad said something about getting folks together to clean up the park, but I like it so full of wild vines and flowers. I just love flowers and plants—even my club token has a flowering vine on it. So, that's me, Aly the Magical Flower Girl!

Rachel Cohen

Hi, I'm Rachel, and I'm wild about animals, especially bears. When we lived in New York, I had to share a room with my twin sister Aly. She's really not into animals, and sometimes we thought we were going to go nuts sharing the same room. Lucky for us, we moved out of that dinky apartment in the city, and snap!—did everything change! Now I have my own room, so I'm going to go animal crazy with the decor. My dad said I can even paint leopard spots all over my dresser if I want to. I'm not really an artist like Aly, but I love animal craft projects so I can definitely turn my room into a wildlife sanctuary.

Our new house here in Connecticut is huge and sometimes a little spooky, but Dad says he'll work out the creaks and moans a little at a time. My dad loves a good DIY project, and I don't mind swinging a hammer sometimes. Aly and Mom have already scoped out the yard for a major gardening project. I just hope they leave it wild enough to attract some animals. I saw a deer standing in the backyard on the night we moved in—you don't see that in the city!

One of the coolest things about our new neighborhood is that all the houses in the neighborhood have girls my age living in them—isn't that cool? So, Aly and I not only have new friends, we've even got a clubhouse where we hang out and make things. All the girls are super creative. We even have club symbols! They came in the mail—and it was a big mystery. They're little metal triangles engraved with our favorite things. Mine has a bear on it, which is just one more reason to believe that this place is going to be totally perfect for us.

Marisol Marquez

Do you like jewelry? If so, we should hang out together because I love jewelry. That's what I mostly make at the clubhouse with the other girls. Oh wait, I'm not doing this right so let me start again. Hi! I'm Marisol and my family just moved to Portal, Connecticut where weird things happen. Not "creepy weird," though. Everything is totally wonderful—but definitely unusual. The best part is having five new friends really fast—and that isn't weird at all. Moving hasn't been so bad because of that.

Do you believe in magic? I didn't until recently, though I liked thinking about it. Now I totally do, and I love it! So, I love jewelry and magic and swimming. I'm a great swimmer. Like a fish—oh, that's really funny because my club token has a river dragon on it. "What's a river dragon?" you ask? You'll find out soon enough.

But, um, where was I? Oh right, we just moved to Portal from Florida, and now we live in this really big, old house. I like it, though I kind of miss the beach, but my mom says we can put in a pool as soon as the twins are a little older. We adopted twin babies from China—isn't that the absolute coolest? They're two now so I'll have to wait awhile on the pool because pools are not the safest thing to have with toddlers around.

So, my family is me and my little brother and sister, and my parents. My dad is a chef at this really fancy restaurant in Hartford. That means we eat some strange things sometimes, but that can be interesting, too. Before we moved, my mom worked in an insurance office but she stays home with us now. She says that having two-year-old twins is work enough.

Kaida Jordan

Hi, I'm Kaida, and I'm almost thirteen so I'm the oldest member of our new club. I'm a little old for the whole "Let's form a club" thing, but I really like hanging out with the girls in the neighborhood. Sometimes I feel like an older sister to the other girls, but that's totally cool. Another thing that's totally cool is the small building in the middle of the park. After we started our club, we kind of took over the building and made it our clubhouse.

We do crafts in the clubhouse. I really like crafts, which is kind of surprising because I'm not real big on just sitting around. I do like to try new things, so I've learned how to do a lot of different crafts. I'm thinking of doing some kind of craft using the picture from my club token—it's a winged unicorn, and it's totally

14

awesome. Anyway, I guess I get my creativity from my mom. She makes really gorgeous pottery using traditional Korean designs and techniques.

My mom says it's good to be well-rounded, which is her way of saying I don't always have to be looking for some new way to break a bone. I love sports, but my mother tries to encourage my creative side. My dad is adventurous like me even though his day job is designing computer software. He and I love going rock climbing, camping, skiing, white-water rafting, etc. together. He even promised to take me hang gliding someday. Mom says she can feel grey hairs growing just thinking about it. Another way I'm well-rounded is ethnically. Mom is Korean, (I bet you guessed that) and Dad is African-American. Our family reunions can be a little weird.

Speaking of weird, our neighborhood is full of mysteries. There is a spooky old park right in the middle of a circle of six totally ancient houses. And, we—my family and our new neighbors—are supposedly the first people who've lived in these houses for years and years—even though they're gorgeous and in perfect shape! Mom says the road is the only new thing around here. I'm convinced that if I keep looking, I'm going to find secret passages in our house or maybe in the old clubhouse. Maybe I'll discover mysteries and magic!

Shaylee Ballard

Bonjour! Je m'appelle Shaylee. That's French. Don't tell the other girls, but one of the reasons I love French is because it's the language of dance. At least, that's how I think of it. So many ballet terms, like plié and relevé, are French, and I think they make ballet sound so pretty. I love dancing, and not just ballet (though that's my favorite)—I love everything about dance in general. My dance teacher says it's important to get a taste of many different forms. So, I want to taste as many forms as I can! I even make up my own dances.

I'm the only one in my neighborhood who likes to dance. I think Kaida would be an awesome dancer, but she's way too busy with sports. Still, my new friends have gotten me to think about something besides dance because they're all into crafts. And I found out I love crafts and creating stuff. I especially like making dance stuff—no surprise there, right? Everyone in our group has a club token. Mine has some kind of fairy on it. I don't think a fairy matches me exactly, but when I look closely—I'm pretty sure she's dancing.

I'm the youngest one in our girls' club, but nobody treats me like a baby there (not like some brothers I could mention). Our girls' club is still pretty new because we all just moved to Connecticut. My family used to live in North Carolina. Of course, we used to live with my dad, too. Now we don't, which is still pretty sad. So, it's just me, my mom and my two teenage brothers. If you ever wish you could have a big brother, let me know. I could be talked into giving you one of mine!

Larissa Delany

Just call me Rissa!

My dad used to be a police detective in Indianapolis, but now he's the Chief of Police here in Portal. At first, I thought I was going to hate moving from a big city to Outer Nowhere, but this place is awesome. Our house is huge—all the houses in the neighborhood are huge, but they aren't like all the boring new McMansions you see in new housing developments. These are really ancient and kind of spooky. I love them.

I also love my new friends. Would you believe a girl my age lives in every house in this neighborhood? Yeah, like that's a coincidence—not! Plus, we're all really creative and we get along great, well, when we're not feeling snarky. Friends hardly ever get along all the time—right? But we're BFF, I know it. Plus, they never tease me about important stuff like how much I love color. I know it sounds kinda weird, but I can't get enough of it—color, that is. I would live in a rainbow if I could. Luckily, my dad says he's fine with my unique style too—as long as I don't do anything permanent! So, I cut my own hair and sometimes change its color on a daily basis. And, all of my clothes are decorated with lots of color. I don't want to look like anyone but me.

We, the neighborhood girls and I, have a club now—mostly we do crafts. Each of us also has a club token, which is totally mysterious. We don't even know where they came from. Mine has a book on it. That probably seems like a weird thing for a someone like me, but I love books. So does my dad. One of the coolest things about our new house is that it has rooms full of built-in bookshelves. I told Dad that I think that's just a challenge! Someday, I might even fill some of those shelves with books I write about my adventures and the adventures I have with the other girls. 'Cause we have adventures that will blow you away!

CHAPTER 1:
Mysterious Presents

"Are you ready to go?" Rachel poked her head into her sister's room and shuddered at the number of plants hanging from the ceiling. They reminded her of an Amazon expedition on the Discovery Channel. Aly (short for Alysa) turned from where she was sketching flowers on the wall.

"Hey, does Mom know you're drawing on the wall?" Rachel asked.

Aly sighed. "Yes, of course Mom knows. I'm going to paint a mural."

"Cool." In their tiny apartment in New York City, they hadn't even been allowed to push tacks into the walls, much less paint pictures on them. It seemed everything had changed when they moved to Portal, Connecticut.

"What's it going to be?"

"A garden with a fountain," Aly said. "I've been dreaming about it."

Rachel glanced at her watch. "You need to dream later. We're going to be late if you don't hurry up." Rachel turned and dashed down the stairs, knowing her sister would follow eventually. She'd given up on getting Aly to live life at more than a snail's pace. They might be identical twins, but they were totally different in many ways. "Mom, we're heading to the clubhouse!"

"Check the mail first," her mom called from inside her office. Just then, Rachel heard a crash that sounded like another pile of books toppling over. The books stacked all over Mom's home office made it look like she was building a model of the Leaning Tower of Pisa out of 10-pound law books.

"OK!" Rachel headed for the mailbox at top speed, opened it and scooped out the contents. To her surprise, there were two small packages—one addressed to her and the other to Aly. She glanced toward the house to see Aly stepping out the front door. She held up the boxes. "We got presents!"

Aly frowned. "Like what? Soap samples?"

Rachel shrugged and tossed Aly her package, then began tearing open her own. She reached into the box and pulled out a small metal triangle. It was a little bigger than a quarter and had a picture of a bear engraved on it. Rachel looked up to see Aly holding a similar triangle. "What do you suppose they are?"

Aly shook her head and shrugged. "Paperweights? They're kind of heavy."

"The bear is cool," Rachel said, rubbing her thumb across the engraving. The grizzly was frozen mid-step as he lumbered across the triangle. She could almost imagine him turning to look at her. Rachel was wild about bears. In her huge stuffed animal collection, she had more than a dozen bears. She had even made a cute bear family out of polymer clay.

Aly held her triangle up. "Mine has a flower." Rachel rolled her eyes.

Just then their mom stepped out onto the porch. "Are you girls going to bring in the mail or just stand around until I come get it?"

The sisters held out their triangles. "This is all there was," Rachel said.

The twins' mom squinted against the sun and walked across the front yard. She looked at the odd triangles, running her finger over the cool metal. "They're pretty. Whoever sent them sure seems to know what you girls like best. Maybe they're something Grandma found on her vacation."

"Grandma would put in a note," Aly said. "Wouldn't she?"

Mom nodded. "Probably, but you never really know with Grandma." She looked at the twins. "I thought you girls were going to the clubhouse."

"*Oh no!*" Rachel screeched, shoving the metal triangle into her pocket and dashing down the sidewalk. "We are *so* late!" For once, even Aly ran to keep up.

The clubhouse was the place where all the girls in the neighborhood met to swap magazines, gobble snacks, work on craft projects and just hang out. It was a small stone building in the middle of the tiny park that sat in the exact center of a ring of six houses. The park was filled with strange statues and surrounded by a high iron fence, and that was just one of the weird things about their new neighborhood.

All six of the houses in the circle were ancient. Rachel's dad said he thought the houses might be more than two hundred years old. Until a couple months ago, all the houses had been empty, maintained for years by some mysterious foundation, and then, *bang!* they'd all been sold to families with kids. Aly and Rachel's parents had bought the last house in the neighborhood at the beginning of the summer.

The foundation still owned the park, though it had become awfully overgrown and weedy. Still, the foundation said anyone who lived in the neighborhood was welcome to use it. All the families had daughters close in age; the girls had taken over the small building in the middle of the park and made it their clubhouse.

When Rachel and Aly reached the clubhouse door, they were panting from the run. As they pushed it open, they were met with a chorus of hellos from the girls sitting around a large wooden table inside.

"Sorry we're late," Rachel said.

"That's OK," Larissa answered. Rachel immediately noticed that Rissa, as the girls had nicknamed her, had given herself another hairstyle. This time it looked like she'd gathered random clumps of hair and dyed each one a different color. Rissa loved temporary hair dye, so the girls never knew what to expect. She gave an exaggerated yawn. "Shaylee was just making us look at another of her scrapbooks."

"No one said you had to look," the petite blonde said, pulling the lacy pink book away from her friend.

Kaida laughed and put down her latest project—a brightly colored cross-stitch picture of a fierce dragon. Kaida was always trying new crafts; she said she liked mastering new things. "Rissa is just miffed because there aren't more photos of her in Shaylee's scrapbook!"

"Well, you know I'm stylin'," Rissa said, hopping up to strike a pose. Rachel grinned at the way Rissa's rainbow hair matched her tie-dyed T-shirt. Rissa had never met a color she didn't like, and she used as many as possible to decorate her clothes and make them as brightly colored as her hair.

Always the peacemaker, Aly slipped into a seat beside Shaylee. "I'd like to see your scrapbook."

Shaylee beamed and opened the book. Rachel glanced at the pages as she slid into a chair. Lots of pink. Lots of ballet photos. Shaylee loved two things: dancing and making crafts about dancing. Right now, she was in a very pink scrapbook phase. "I see the problem, Rissa," Rachel said with a grin. "You need to wear more pink."

"*As if,*" Rissa said, but then she leaned over to get a closer look. "I don't see any pictures of Jacob and Connor," she said.

Shaylee sniffed. "I see my brothers enough in person.

This morning they're putting an ugly basketball hoop above the garage door. They woke me up with all the nail pounding—nobody needs to pound nails before 9 a.m.!"

"You should get a portable goal," Kaida said. "Like ours. That way you can take it down or move it if you need to."

"Do they make them in pink?" Rissa asked.

Rachel slouched down in her chair as she listened to her friends tease each other. Then, remembering the odd present from the afternoon mail, she dug through her pockets and pulled out the heavy triangle. "Hey, look at the cool thing I got in the mail today. Aly got one too."

"I got one of those today too," Marisol said. She pulled over her huge tote bag and began rooting through it, the bracelets on her arm tinkling like wind chimes. Marisol was seriously into jewelry—if she wasn't making it, she was buying it. "Mine has a different picture though."

"Mine too," Rissa said. She held out a triangle with a book carved into it. Rachel was secretly glad she hadn't gotten a boring picture like that. So far, she definitely liked hers best.

"Mine has some kind of fairy or elf. It's in there," Shaylee said, nodding toward her own bag, a pale pink canvas tote with fuchsia ballerinas in different poses stamped all over on the front and back.

Marisol finally whooped in triumph, "Found it!" and pulled out her triangle. It had the weirdest picture of all, like a cross between a dragon and mermaid with a long snout and lots of wavy fins. "I don't know what it is, but it's very cool. I love mermaids."

Kaida leaned forward to put her elbows on the table, and held out a triangle with a winged unicorn on it. "I bet I'm the only one who knows what these are."

"Paperweights?" Aly suggested.

"Magnets," Kaida answered. "I tried it on our fridge."

Aly frowned. "But they're so heavy."

"It's a pretty strong magnet. I had to pry it off with a butter knife."

"It's cool that we all have one," Rissa said. "They could be our club emblem or something." She flipped her magnet in the air like a coin and tried to catch it, but just missed. The triangle hit the table with a dull *thunk*—and stuck. "Hey, what kind of magnet sticks to a wooden table?"

"That's weird." Kaida placed her triangle on the table, then gasped as her triangle scooted across the table until one of its points touched Rissa's triangle. When it stopped moving, it seemed to be stuck fast to the table, just like Rissa's. "Definitely freaky!"

CHAPTER 2:
The Secret Portal Opens

The girls stared at the two triangles on the table. Kaida reached out and tried to nudge one, but it was stuck. "You'd think I could slide it a little," she said.

"Well, magnets have poles," Rachel said, remembering something from her science class. "That's probably what made them move by themselves, and, if they're really strong magnets, they could be really trying to keep those poles touching." Her voice trailed off a little as she added. "But magnets definitely aren't attracted to wood."

"Maybe the table is magical," Marisol said, smiling.

"Oh yeah, that's *got* to be it," Rissa laughed.

Marisol grinned. "OK, maybe the table's made of metal sandwiched between wood?"

"And those dinky magnets are sticking that hard right

through the wood?" Kaida asked. "I still say that it's seriously freaky."

Rachel put her triangle on the table near the other two, and it also slid until it touched only one point of Kaida's triangle. Without saying anything, Marisol and Aly added theirs and watched them slide into place, making a rough circle with one empty spot.

"Where's yours?" Rissa asked Shaylee. Shaylee rummaged through her bag until she found it. She laid it on the table at least six inches from the other pieces, and it practically flew into place. The six triangles had formed a circle. Then, suddenly, the circle of wooden table between the triangles vanished, and the girls could see through the table. But they didn't see the worn gray carpet of the clubhouse floor. Instead, they saw dirt and moss and rock.

"Whoa!" Rissa breathed.

Rachel ducked down and looked under the table to see if there was a hole in the floor, but the floor looked perfectly normal, as did the underside of the table. Whatever they were looking at through the hole, *it wasn't really there.*

"It looks like you could reach right in," Marisol said in an awed voice.

"Yeah, sure, I would totally stick my hand in there— *never!*" Rissa shook her head so that hard a clump of purple hair fell over her eyes.

Kaida leaned forward, chewing on her lip as she stared into the hole. Then she unclipped a barrette from her thick black hair and tossed it into the hole. It fell to the ground below. They watched it bounce off a rock before landing in a patch of moss. "It's a real hole!" Kaida exclaimed.

"I vote we all go home now," Shaylee said, scooting her chair away from the table.

Rissa looked at her. "You can go home if you want, but I want to see what this is."

Shaylee's lip crept out as if she might cry, and Aly slipped an arm around her. "If you're scared, I'll go with you," Aly said. Shaylee shivered slightly, but she shook her head.

Just then a girl's face appeared in the hole, looking as if she were twisting nearly upside down to peer up at the girls above the table. Shaylee screamed and jumped back from the table, knocking over her chair. The face vanished.

"OK, I'm definitely ready to go home now," Shaylee said to Aly, backing away from the table so quickly she nearly tripped. By now, all the girls were on their feet, and clearly Shaylee wasn't the only one who thought leaving might be a good idea.

Then the face popped up again, but this time, it appeared that the strange girl had stepped under the table and thrust her hands through the hole and somehow pushed the hole open to make it bigger. A second later, her head popped through the hole. She squirmed a bit and the hole grew large enough for her to pull herself through to the shoulders and then to the waist. Then she pulled herself up so that she was sitting on the edge of the hole in the table with her legs dangling into it. She didn't look scary, but seeing her wiggling up out of hole in a solid wood table in their ordinary old clubhouse was too much for all of the girls, and they ran for the door.

"Don't go, Princesses!" the strange girl begged. "Please don't go." She reached out a hand beseechingly.

Aly stopped, her hand still holding the handle of the half-open door. "Princesses?"

Rissa was the first to take a small step back toward the table. "Who are you?" she asked. "*What* are you?"

One look showed that the girl was *something* unusual. Her skin had a slightly green tint, and she had dark green hair—if you could call it hair. Her head looked like it was covered with downy green feathers that lay close to her head, exposing finely-pointed ears. Her slightly slanted eyes were green as well. "I am Eidermoss of the Folk, Princess. We need your help. Please, please, don't go!"

"You need our help?" Kaida replied, crossing her arms and frowning. "Help with what?"

"You have to open the Wellspring," Eidermoss begged. "Only the Princesses can restore the magic!"

"Um, we don't know anything about magic," Rachel said.

"Except what we've read about in books," Marisol added, "and seen in movies."

"And we are not princesses," Rissa said firmly. "I didn't even do the princess thing when I was little!"

The strange girl looked at her in astonishment. "Oh, you *are* a princess. You are Larissa, Princess of Spellcraft." She turned toward Shaylee and spoke softly, as if awed. "And you are Shaylee, Princess of the Folk." She bowed her head slightly. "We have waited so long for the Princesses to open the door. Without the fresh flow of magic, my people are weak. My world is dying." Her voice rose shrilly. "We don't even *dance* anymore. You are all Princesses. Please, come and help!"

"You want us to climb through the hole in the table?" Shaylee asked.

Eidermoss looked down at the tabletop. "It would be easier if you had put the realm keys on a wall."

"They're stuck," Rissa said. "Besides, we didn't know they were keys. They didn't exactly come with instructions."

"Can you climb through?" Eidermoss asked anxiously.

Rissa put her hands on her hips. "Not *can* we—the question is *will* we."

"I will," Kaida said. "I'll help. Besides, you've got to admit, this has to be the biggest adventure in Connecticut today!" She scrambled up onto the table and Eidermoss smiled. Kaida turned back toward the others. "Anyone else want to play extreme princesses?"

Rachel shrugged. "I'm game."

One by one, each of the girls agreed. Aly held Shaylee's hand for courage when it was their turn to crawl up onto the table and slip down through the hole. It required some undignified wiggling to get through the hole, but soon they all stood in a small wooded clearing.

"Where's the hole?" Rachel yelped. It had vanished after the last girl was through.

"There isn't enough magic to hold it open on this side," Eidermoss said. "And now that you've left your world, there isn't enough magic to hold it open there, either."

"You mean we're stuck here?" Shaylee wailed.

"Oh, no, Princess. Once you find the Wellspring and release the magic, you can open the hole, or door, again."

"So we can only get home again if we succeed?" Rissa asked.

Eidermoss opened her eyes very wide. "Yes, I think so."

CHAPTER 3:
The Guardians

The girls stood silently for a moment, absorbing the fact that they were trapped. Rachel shuddered. Adventures seemed a lot more fun when you watched them on television—in real life, they were just scary.

"Once again, it really would have helped if this adventure thing had come with instructions or at least a map," Rissa said. Then she sighed. "Are you going to tell us where to find the Wellspring?"

Eidermoss shook her head. "I do not know where it is, Princess. Only the Guardians know."

"Great," Rissa said. She dropped her voice and muttered, "Who wants to bet the Guardians are drooling two-headed monsters?"

Rachel glanced at Aly, who was acting a bit strange.

Ever since she'd stepped into the clearing, Aly had been turning around slowly, looking at the trees. "What's up, Aly?" Rachel asked.

"Everything is glowing." She kept turning, eyes wide in amazement. "Why is everything glowing?"

"You are Alysa, Princess of the Earth," Eidermoss said, her tone puzzled. "You see the energy of all things. It's part of your magic."

"Not usually," Rachel said.

"It's beautiful," Aly breathed.

Suddenly the girls heard movement in the forest shadows. "Friends of yours?" Rissa asked Eidermoss.

The green girl shook her head hard. "No, the Guardians are coming."

Six huge grizzly bears lumbered into the clearing. Their fur was almost golden, and they were as big as Clydesdales. Just as the girls were turning to run, the largest bear stopped, as did the others behind him.

"Welcome, Princess."

Rachel was shocked to hear the bear's deep, gruff voice in her head. "Um, thank you."

"I am Fleet, leader of the Guardians. Have you come to restore the magic?" the bear asked.

"I guess," Rachel said. Then, speaking more firmly, she added, "We'll try."

"Why are you talking to the bear?" Rissa hissed loudly.

"He spoke first."

"I didn't hear anything," Aly said.

"Me neither," chimed in Shaylee. The others nodded

their heads in agreement.

"Well, I don't exactly hear him," Rachel said. "His words are kind of in my head. I know that sounds really weird, but that's the best way I can explain it."

"That's what I thought," Rissa snorted. Aly glared at her.

"The Guardians can only be heard by you," Fleet said to Rachel. "You are Princess of the Guarded Forest. We have come to take you and your companions to the Wellspring of Magic. We are the Guardians."

Rachel turned and told the others what the bear had said. The other girls still looked at her in half disbelief, and half amazement.

"Are they *really* the Guardians?" Rissa asked, turning toward Eidermoss. The green girl was trembling and didn't speak; she only nodded.

"Well, at least they aren't drooling. I guess we should go with them," Rissa sighed.

"They're awfully big." Shaylee was trembling nearly as hard as Eidermoss.

"But they're amazing," Marisol added softly.

"Will you go with us?" Rachel asked Eidermoss.

"Oh, no, Princess," Eidermoss whimpered.

"Why not?" Rachel asked.

"The Folk rarely enter the Guarded Forest. I only came this time because we could feel the change—we knew you were coming, and because I hoped I would not see the Guardians." Eidermoss spoke so softly that the girls had to lean close to hear her. "Everyone knows that the Guardians eat people."

Shaylee shrieked, "I am *not* going with them! I want to go home—*now!*"

Eidermoss grew more agitated. "No, Princess! Save us, please!"

Through the high-pitched chatter, Rachel heard Fleet's deep voice in her head. "Have no fear, Princess. We do not eat the silly Meadow Dancers. Those tales are from their imaginations only."

"Fleet says they won't eat you," Rachel said. "If we want to get home, it looks like going with the bears is the only way we'll get there."

Shaylee pointed at Eidermoss. "If she's not going, I'm not going either."

Eidermoss shook like a leaf, but she stammered, "If my Princess requires I go, I will go."

There was a new burst of hysteria when Shaylee and Eidermoss found out that the bears intended for the girls to ride on their broad backs in order to move through the forest more quickly. Despite Fleet's assurances, Eidermoss obviously thought she was not going to survive the day.

"What if Eidermoss and Shaylee stayed here?" Rachel suggested. "The rest of us could go and do whatever needs to be done."

The Guardian shook his huge, grizzly head. "No, the Princess of the Folk must lead the dance during the calling of the magic."

Rachel relayed Fleet's message to the others.

"Dance?" Shaylee said. The younger girl sounded calm

for the first time since entering the realm. "Did he really say there's a dance?"

The bear looked at Shaylee, though he still spoke only in Rachel's head. Rachel passed his words on. "The dance comes from inside you, Princess of the Folk. It is part of *your* magic, as is all creativity. When the time comes, it will flow out of you like the magic of the Wellspring, and all of the Princesses will join you in dance."

Shaylee looked nervously at the huge bear, then nodded slowly. "OK, I'll come." She turned to Eidermoss, who stood beside her, trembling and whimpering. Shaylee patted her arm. "You don't have to come. My friends will be there with me."

Eidermoss gushed her thanks like a broken faucet even while the girls climbed up onto the bears' broad backs. Honeyglow, the smallest of the bears, had to lie nearly flat in order for Shaylee to scramble up onto her back. Finally, the bears turned and lumbered back into the woods with the girls clinging tightly.

Fleet's rolling gait made it a challenge to hold on. Rachel had ridden horses a few times at summer camp, but found riding the bear much more difficult. "If you lay close against me," Fleet said, "you should find riding easier."

Rachel passed on the suggestion to the others, and soon the girls were riding flat on their stomachs. They still clutched handfuls of fur, but the new position definitely felt more secure.

"Is it far?" Rachel asked Fleet.

"No," the bear answered. "The Wellspring is at the exact center of the forest. We are nearly to the forest's heart."

"What happens when we get to the Wellspring?"

"The Guardians cannot go the whole way with you. The Garden of the Wellspring is now protected even from us. When the forest sensed that the Wellspring was damaged, it closed its heart to all but the Princesses. Once you enter the heart of the forest, you will need to use your magic to restore the spring."

"But I don't have any magic," Rachel argued. "None of us does."

"You are already using your magic," he answered. "Have you not noticed?" Rachel felt a rumble of something like laughter from the bear.

"You mean by talking to you?"

Fleet nodded. "Do not fret, Princess. When the time comes, the magic you need will come too."

"How can we have magic if the magical well thingie is broken?" Rachel insisted.

Again she felt the rumble of the bear's laughter. "Your magic is different and cannot be blocked by anyone or anything as long as you use the creative talents inside you. That is why you are Princesses."

"That's another question," Rachel said. "Exactly why are *we* the Princesses? We're just regular girls."

Rachel felt a shrug ripple across the bear's back. "There are many questions I cannot answer. I am only a Guardian."

"Swell," Rachel muttered.

They made the rest of the trip in silence. Rachel was glad they were able to ride, as nothing proved to be much of an obstacle to the huge bears. They never had to hurry or put forth a lot of effort. It was like riding on big, furry tanks that barreled through thickets as easily as walking down an open path. Finally, the bears stopped.

"Are we at the Wellspring?" Kaida asked.

"This is as as close to the Wellspring as the Guardians are allowed," Fleet said.

Rachel slid off the bear's back, landing lightly on her feet. She explained to the others that they would have to go the rest of the way without the bears.

Kaida frowned. "Which way would that be?"

Fleet pointed with his broad muzzle. "Through there."

Rachel turned to look. Ahead of them was a wall of thick vines, rising high into the trees and offering no entrance whatsoever. A mouse might make it through, but not an 11-year-old girl.

"Through *there?*" Rachel asked in disbelief. "We're supposed to get in through *there?* Well, that's the end of this adventure! You need to show us another way in."

CHAPTER 4:
The First Spell

The great golden bear shook his head. "It is the way," he said firmly. "Do not give up so easily."

"What's he saying?" Marisol asked.

Rachel pointed. "He said that's the way to the Wellspring."

"There's no 'way' there," Rissa said, walking over to the thick wall of vines. "It's a wall."

"It is the way," Fleet insisted.

Rachel sighed and shrugged. "He says it's the way."

Soon all the girls were standing at the wall of vines, trying to peer through the thick greenery. "I'm pretty little," Shaylee said, "and I couldn't get through there. We had better see if there's a way around this."

Fleet turned toward the other bears. "We must go now."

"Wait, we need to find another way in!" Rachel shouted at the bears' retreating backs. "Stop! Um, I *command* you as Princess!"

Fleet whirled and bared long sharp teeth, making the girls jump back. "You are Princesses, but you do not command *me!*"

"*Sorry,*" Rachel said meekly, "but there's just no way we can get through there."

"It is the way," Fleet repeated. He turned away, and the Guardians lumbered toward the tree line. Without another glance at the girls, they disappeared into the woods.

"Oh, we're *much* better off now," Rissa said. "Too bad none of us thought to bring our magic machete."

"I'd rather have an enchanted chainsaw," Kaida commented as she leaned closer to the vines and began tugging on them. "We're not getting through here."

"Fleet said each of us has some kind of magic to do this," Rachel said. "We just have to figure out which of us has the right magic for this."

"I could try dancing," Shaylee said. "Rachel said Fleet mentioned dancing."

"You could try," Marisol said. "I'll dance with you."

Shaylee took a few tentative steps that Marisol repeated. Soon, Rachel and Rissa had joined in; but there was no sign of a change in the hedge of vines. "Come and do it with us," Rachel suggested, calling to the other two.

Soon the six girls were dancing in unison. They repeated the simple dance over and over until Rachel was sweaty from the exercise and the humid forest air. "It's not working," she said.

"It must be someone else's magic," Marisol panted, "and we don't even know what kind of 'princesses' we're all supposed to be!"

"But," Rachel said thoughtfully, "we do know what kind of princess Rissa is supposed to be. It was something about spells, right?"

All the girls smiled. "Right!"

"The only problem is that I have no idea how you do a spell," Rissa said.

"On television," Shaylee said, "spells always rhyme, and you write poetry, so maybe you're supposed to make up a rhyme for this."

Rissa shrugged. "I could try." She scrunched her face in thought for a minute, then said, "We fly up, we slip under, we walk right through—I really don't care which thing we do." Rissa paused, thinking. Kaida frowned and made a rolling motion with her hand to get Rissa going again.

Rissa made a face at her and said. "Magic move us—we need some luck. Get us out of here, 'cause we're so stuck!" She nodded and grinned at the other girls.

Rachel turned to look at the thick wall of vines and held her breath. Would Rissa's spell get them through? Would it do anything at all?

Suddenly a gust of wind swept down into the small clearing and spun around the girls, kicking up bits of leaves and dirt. It was like being surrounded by a small tornado. "Did I do this?" Rissa shrieked.

Kaida yelled something back but the howling wind drowned out the sound of her voice. Shaylee shrieked as the spinning wind shrank around the girls and lifted them off the ground. Surprisingly, the wind didn't spin them, but only lifted them gently and carried them out of the clearing. For a moment, Rachel thought it would drop them safely on the other side of the wall of vines. Instead, they flew through the air, past the forest entirely and far away from the Wellspring.

Kaida whooped as they rushed through the air, and Rachel saw that even Shaylee was smiling slightly. They were flying! The view of the flashing treetops from the air was thrilling. After a minute or so, the girls could see a river below. Then they noticed that they were losing speed and beginning to swoop down.

"I can't swim!" Shaylee yelled.

Marisol put an arm around the younger girl. "I can! I'll keep you safe."

But the wind carried them just past the edge of the river before dumping them in a swampy clearing. The trees surrounding the clearing were twisted and sickly looking, and the ground was an odd, multicolored, muddy slush.

"I'm sinking!" Rachel shouted as the mushy ground under her feet gave way.

"Me too!" Aly yelled. A chorus of cries made it clear that they all were sinking.

"It's quicksand!" Rissa exclaimed.

"I don't think so," Marisol said. "It's more like squishy mud." She reached out to catch hold of Shaylee's hand.

"Stop fighting it. It's like swimming. Struggling will make you sink quicker."

"Well, like I said when I thought we were about to be dropped in the river, I can't swim! And this is so gross," Shaylee whimpered, wiping at a glob of mud on her arm.

The girls sank until they were nearly waist-deep in the gooey mud, then they stopped. They were stuck fast but not sinking anymore.

"You just had to put 'stuck' in your spell," Kaida snapped at Rissa.

"You want me to try again?" Rissa asked.

"No!" the girls shouted in unison.

Rachel looked around. Though the trees seemed to lean in toward them slightly, none of the branches was within reach. "How come there's no useful vine hanging around? There's always a useful vine in the movies."

"Yeah, well, there's popcorn at the movies too," Kaida said, "and I'm not seeing any of that either."

"Hush!" Aly hissed. "We're not alone!"

"What?" Rachel turned toward her sister so sharply that she nearly fell forward into the muck. "What do you mean? 'We're not alone'?"

"I see something moving through the trees," Aly said, "or the energy from it anyway. I think maybe it's a person."

"Hey, great!" Rissa said. "Help! Help! We're stuck!"

A little boy stepped into the clearing. His skin was faintly green, but every bit that the girls could see was striped with mud. He wore a thin leather hat pulled low on his forehead, and he looked to be no more than 6 or 7 years old. "What are you doing in our source?" he demanded.

Kaida crossed her arms and glared. "We heard mud was a great beauty treatment so we just rushed over."

"We're stuck," Marisol said, smiling sweetly. "Can you help us?"

The boy peered closely at them. "You look funny. What are you?"

"We're Princesses," Rissa said. When the boy laughed, she frowned and pointed at Shaylee. "She is the Princess of the Folk!"

"If you are the Princesses," the boy said, "why are you here? The Wellspring is not fixed—everyone would know if it was, and this is not the Guarded Forest."

Kaida snorted. "Blame the Princess of Spellcraft. She rhymed us into the mud."

"Hey," Rissa retorted. "It was my first spell, OK?"

"You do not act like Princesses," the boy said. "You act like my sisters." His tone of voice made it clear that he wasn't paying them a compliment.

"We look a lot more regal when we're not stuck in the mud," Rachel assured him. "So would you mind helping us? Please?"

"I will ask the others," the boy said. Then he turned and disappeared back into the gloomy trees before they could call to him.

"Great," Kaida said. "Well, I know I'm having a good time. Especially now that I can't feel my feet." The cold mud was beginning to make all the girls shiver.

Suddenly Rachel spotted movement in one of the trees

close to the edge of the muddy pit. It seemed to be leaning toward Aly. "Look out!" she yelled. "I think that tree's going to fall!"

"No," Aly said. "It's not." The tree leaned still closer and one of the branches actually bent down toward Aly's reaching hands.

"Are you doing that?" Rachel asked, stunned.

"Yes," Aly said as she finally grabbed the branch and wrapped her arms around it. "I guess it's one of my Princess powers. I can talk to the tree." She closed her eyes and leaned her face against the rough bark of the tree branch. The tree began slowly standing upright again and the girls could see Aly inching out of the mud.

She was still about thigh deep in the sticky mud when the girls heard an ominous crack. "The branch is breaking!" Rachel yelled.

"It's too hard for the tree to pull me out," Aly said. "I need to let go! I'm hurting it!" She unwrapped her arms from around the branch, but it curled around her, and the tree kept tugging. "No!" Aly yelled, slapping at the branch. "You have to let go—your branch will break!"

They heard another loud crack, and the girls could see where the branch was splitting off the tree. But the tree still continued to straighten, pulling steadily against the grip of the mud.

When Aly was only knee deep in the mud, the branch broke free completely. "Aly!" Rachel yelled, straining against the mire toward her sister. The thick branch brushed her arm as it crashed into the mud. Rachel yelled again. "Aly!"

CHAPTER 5:
The Mud Shapers

Rachel leaned across the mud and began tugging at the end of the branch, while shouting her sister's name.

"I'm OK," Aly gasped. "Just a little winded. I think I can climb out of the mud using the branch."

Rachel felt tears of relief begin to flow when her sister's mud-streaked face appeared above the branch. Aly slowly crawled up onto the branch and began inching along it toward the edge of the mud pit. Finally, she was able to stand up, albeit shakily. She looked more like a mud pie than a girl—but at least she was standing.

Just then, a small group of mud-streaked people stepped out of the gloom. "Princess of the Earth," an older man said formally to Aly as the whole group bowed slightly. "We are the Mud Shapers Folk. We saw the tree heed your magic. We have come to help as well."

Using the broken branch as a makeshift bridge, several of the people got close enough to the girls to slip a rope around each of them, placing it under their arms. Using the thick trunk of the tree that had helped Aly, they pulled at the ropes. Even the tree seemed to lean slightly away from the muck, as if doing its part to help pull. One by one, the girls were hauled from the mud's grip—each one popping free with a wet *plop*.

As the muddy girls stood together, the small group bowed again. "We are honored, Princesses." A thin man with dots of mud speckling his bald head in a leopard-print pattern bowed nearly to the ground. "We apologize for our slowness in rescue—young Stripe did not recognize you. We are far away from the rest of the Folk and news travels slowly."

"Th-that's OK," Shaylee chattered.

"Enough with the speeches, Spindlethorne!" An older lady with elaborate swirls of dried mud on each cheek pushed through the crowd and gathered the girls close to her. "Can't you see the Princesses are frozen through? We can bow and chatter once we get them in dry clothes and filled up with hot soup."

Rachel thought that sounded wonderful. The girls gladly let the bossy woman hustle them down a narrow path between the twisted trees. Along the way, they learned that the woman's name was Hearth. "They sure give people strange names here," Rachel thought, but her teeth chattered too much for conversation, so she just let the flood of comforting words flow over her. She was glad of the woman's protective arms because her feet were still numb with cold and she stumbled over every root in the trail. After Shaylee nearly fell several times, a brawny man simply scooped her up and carried the tiny girl the rest of the way.

The Folk led the girls into a large mud-brick building. Rachel nearly cried with joy when the warmth of the room enveloped her. Hearth pushed a bowl of hot soup into each girl's hands, and then called for the Folk men to fill wooden tubs with hot water before shooing them out so the Princesses could bathe.

Rachel had been to a lot of slumber parties in her 11 years, but this was her first bath party—and the hot water was to die for. Hearth insisted that the girls stay in the tubs until their fingers were as wrinkly as raisins. Then she produced soft, warm dresses and cloaks for each of them.

"This is lovely," Marisol said, stroking her velvety blue-green cloak. "But my mom will kill me if I don't bring home my regular clothes."

Hearth was horrified. "Plain dwellers kill their children?" she gasped.

"No, that's just a saying," Marisol reassured her. "She would yell at me a lot, though, if she saw my clothes so dirty."

"Oh, have no concern, Princess," Hearth said, patting Marisol's hand. "I will have the clothes cleaned." She began bustling around, picking up the girls' muddy things.

Rachel knew the steamy bath would quickly turn her curly hair into a lion's mane, so she pulled it back into a ponytail and looked for something to tie around it. Hearth quickly saw her problem and braided Rachel's hair tightly enough to turn up the corners of her eyes before tying a bit of leather around the bottom.

During the impromptu hairdressing session, the other girls wandered around the room. The large room had fireplaces at either end. In one, cooking pots were hanging over the fire, but the other was nearly enclosed with bricks. "Is this where you bake bread?" Aly asked.

"Oh no, Princess," the older woman said. "That is where we bake the beads."

Marisol turned sharply to look toward the enclosed fireplace. "You make beads?" she asked excitedly.

Hearth smiled. "Would you like to look?"

The girls gathered around as the older woman took down tray after tray of incredibly beautiful clay beads. In one tray, each bead was a swirl of rainbow colors. In another, the beads were tiny pink roses, positioned with their petals open to show their golden hearts. Another tray held oblong beads so black that they glowed blue in the firelight. "They're beautiful!" Kaida gasped.

"That is what we do," Hearth said softly. "We coax the beauty from the clay and marry it to the magic that each will do."

"Who would guess that the gunk all over our clothes could turn into these?" Rissa said.

"Often what is plainest on the outside hides the greatest treasure," Hearth said. "I should let the others in now." She padded over to open the wide wooden doors and soon the room was filled with smiling people—all with different intricate mud patterns painted on their green skin.

"Ah," said the balding man, Spindlethorne. "Hearth has shown you our treasure and our duty."

"Are these beads really magical?" Rachel asked. "What do they do?"

The man ran his fingers through the unique beads on one of the trays, his face wistful. "They hold little magic now," he said. "But these beads are the first gift to every Folk child born."

Marisol looked alarmed. "They look like a choking hazard to me." She had 2-year-old twin siblings at home and sometimes launched into mom-like lectures about child safety.

Spindlethorne smiled warmly at her. "We've never had a baby eat one yet."

"What do they do with them?" Marisol asked.

"When a child is born, the parents choose a bead that represents the gifting they see in the child." He held up several beads. "The rose is for sensitivity to nature. The rainbow is for exuberant joy. The beads are strung on a leather cord and tied to the child's ankle. It serves as a kind of protection and a reminder of their gifts and abilities."

"It sounds like a beautiful tradition," Rachel said. "Too bad we don't do it back home. I could use a little magic during math class."

"I do not know about math class," Spindlethorne said, "but I believe we can extend the tradition of bead-giving to our Princesses. Your first time in our world is like a kind of birth."

"Wow," Marisol's eyes lit up. "You mean we get one of these beautiful beads?"

The older man nodded. "We will also share our mud with you, so that you are part of our family—our clan."

The girls looked at one another. They felt like they'd already shared quite a bit of mud, but they didn't want to hurt anyone's feelings. The Folk had been so kind. "You honor us," Aly said.

All of the Folk gathered around the girls in a circle near the trays of beads. Spindlethorne asked the Princesses to line up. Then he walked to the first in line—Shaylee—and put his hand on her head. "We welcome Shaylee, Princess of the Folk. Who sees for Shaylee?"

"I do." A slender young woman stepped forward and walked to the trays of beads. She peered into them for a moment, then selected a perfectly round bead swirled with different shades of pink and lavender. "I choose morning sky to remind our dear Princess to embrace new beginnings." She slipped the bead on a leather thong. Then she touched it to Shaylee's forehead before tying it around her ankle.

"It's so beautiful," Shaylee whispered.

Then Hearth handed the young woman a small bowl of thin purplish mud and a tiny brush. The woman painted a triangle on Shaylee's cheek, then painted a careful drawing of a person. Rachel recognized it as the picture on Shaylee's realm key and was amazed that the woman could do such delicate work with mud.

Then Spindlethorne stepped up to Marisol. "We

welcome Marisol, Princess of the Living Waters." Marisol gasped, and then grinned. All the girls knew that Marisol loved swimming and any kind of ocean-themed decorating stuff, so her title fit her perfectly. "Who sees for Marisol?"

Another young woman stepped forward and picked a blue-green bead in the shape of a shell. "I choose hidden treasures to remind you to look deeply and wisely, to know that the way things appear is not always the way they are." Then she accepted a bowl of thin greenish mud and painted the dragon design from Marisol's key on her cheek.

One by one, each of the girls was given a bead and a design intricately done in mud. Rachel smiled when she was given a golden bead in the shape of a bear's head to represent strength without aggression. "Sometimes, it is when we withhold our strength that we use it best," said the woman who chose Rachel's bead.

At Rissa's turn, an elderly man gave her a faceted bead swirled with abstract colors and shapes. He told her it represented discernment and cautioned her to see clearly through the storms of life.

Kaida's chooser turned out to be the burly man who had carried Shaylee so easily through the woods. He chose a shield-shaped bead with a sun so bright in the middle it seemed to glow. "You are Kaida, Princess of the Bright Sky. With great power and strength," he warned, "come greater responsibility. Only by taming the fire can you avoid being consumed." Kaida shivered a bit, looking puzzled.

Finally, Hearth chose for Aly. The leaf-shaped bead in

shades of green was no surprise to anyone. "Just as plants need light," Hearth said softly, "so should you, Princess of the Earth, step out of the shadows and let your quiet power nourish others."

The smiling Folk gathered to hug the girls and welcome them into their community. "You will always have a place here," Spindlethorne said.

"Thank you all," Rachel said. "We're very grateful, but we have a place back home with our families, too, and I don't think we're going to get back there until we finish our quest."

"Can you help us get back to the Wellspring?" Kaida asked.

"There is an overland route we take each spring to trade with our Meadow Folk kin, but it is long and slow," Spindlethorne said. "Far too slow with the magic waning so quickly. Already some of our older folk have become bedridden with the weakness. I believe the only way to get to the Wellspring in time is by river."

The Folk around him gasped, and the girls looked around nervously. "Is there something wrong with going by river?" Marisol asked.

"Monsters," a willow-thin girl said in a low murmur.

"Monsters?" Shaylee squeaked. "I don't really want to meet any monsters."

"Don't be scared." Stripe pushed his way through the crowd and peered up at the girls. "I'll be with you."

"I feel safer already," Rissa mumbled.

"Stripe is the only one among us who has much useful

knowledge of the river," Spindlethorne said. "He has a strong boat and has explored much—to the annoyance of his mother. He will guide you on your trip."

Rachel looked into Stripe's proud, smiling face and hoped they weren't about to sail into total disaster.

CHAPTER 6:
Where Dragons Lurk

It seemed everyone in the entire Mud Shapers' village walked with the girls to the makeshift dock at the edge of the slow-moving river. The dock was really more of a small raft lashed to thick trees at the water's edge. Stripe's boat was tied up at the end of the dock. The boat looked like a cross between a canoe and a raft, with curving sides and a wide, flat bottom. Stripe grinned as the girls looked at it. "My father made it. He was a Sea-goer before he met my mother. This is a great boat—nothing can sink it!"

"Ah, no boasting now, Stripe," scolded Hearth. "No need to invite trouble—especially on the river."

"It looks solid enough," Kaida said.

"It's beautiful," Marisol sighed with a dreamy look on

her face. She walked to the boat and climbed in, staring out at the river with a smile.

"I don't know that I'd go *that* far," Kaida muttered.

"Can you tell us more about the monsters?" Rachel asked. "Have you actually seen monsters in the river?"

"No," Spindlethorne said firmly. "The Monsters come mostly from stories wedded to reports of odd sounds and sights. I believe some Folk are prone to being a little overly imaginative."

"I've seen the monsters," Stripe said cheerily. "They're like snakes, only 10 times longer than my boat. They have fangs as long as my leg, and when they roar, it makes the water boil."

"Right." Kaida rolled her eyes.

"You never know," Shaylee said. "We've seen such weird things here."

"I believe Stripe has an admirable imagination," Spindlethorne said. "But you must not let him frighten you, Princess. It is important that you reach the Wellspring."

The girls couldn't argue with that. Until they accomplished their mission, they couldn't go home. Rachel took a deep breath, grabbed her sister's hand and marched over to the boat, climbing in to sit beside Marisol.

When all the Princesses had taken their seats, Hearth stepped forward and handed Aly a blanket-wrapped parcel. "Your clothes, clean and dry," Hearth said, her eyes twinkling. "We had enough magic left to see to it that your parents do not kill you."

"Thank you," Aly said warmly.

Stripe nearly squirmed with joy as he hopped in, rocking the boat alarmingly. He waved at the small crowd of Folk on the riverbank. They all looked so worried that Rachel felt a small lurch in her stomach that had nothing to do with the bobbing boat.

Stripe cast off the rope that held his boat to the dock and began paddling upstream. The current in the slow-moving river offered little resistance, and the boat moved off slowly but steadily.

"Can I help paddle?" Kaida asked, picking up a second oar from the floor of the boat. "I've had lots of practice paddling canoes at summer camp."

Stripe frowned for a moment, then nodded. "OK, but be careful. If you don't stroke evenly, we'll spin in circles." Kaida dug in with her paddle, and soon the little boat was moving at a fairly steady clip. They were quickly out of sight of the small dock.

The riverbank looked wild and overgrown. Low-hanging limbs hung out over the water. Several times, Stripe and Kaida had to steer around the dangling branches.

Rachel tapped Marisol on the arm. "Are you OK?"

Marisol turned slowly to look at Rachel. Her eyes looked oddly unfocused, as if her mind was far away. "It's so ... Don't you just want to jump into the river?"

Rachel glanced over the side into the water. It was nearly opaque with river silt. "No, actually. It doesn't exactly look appealing," she admitted. "And I bet it's really cold." But Marisol had already turned her attention back to the water. She didn't seem to be listening to Rachel at all.

Turning toward her sister, Rachel whispered, "Marisol is acting really weird. Do you think she's sick?"

Aly bit her lip thoughtfully, then shook her head. "Do you remember when we first got here? I could feel the life-glow from the trees, from the animals, even from you, and it made me want to laugh and just soak it up. It was a while before I could really concentrate." She nodded toward Marisol. "At the bead ceremony, they said Marisol was the Princess of the Living Waters, so maybe she's feeling something like that with the water. I think she'll be OK in a little while."

Rachel hoped so. She didn't remember Aly acting that flaky, but maybe she hadn't noticed then. So much had been going on.

Her thoughts were interrupted when Kaida asked Stripe, "It sounds like there are a few different groups of Folk—Meadow Dancers, Mud Shapers and Sea-goers. Are there any others?"

Stripe shrugged. "I have only seen the Meadow Dancers once, and I have never been to visit my father's people. I have heard of the Spellmasters, but I have never met any. Most Folk are afraid of them."

Rissa perked up when Stripe mentioned spells. "Do you know where the Spellmasters live?"

"On the far side of the Guarded Forest, I think," Stripe said. "It's not near where we're going."

"That's too bad," Kaida said. "Sounds like they might be able to help you with your spells, Rissa."

"I only tried the one spell," Rissa said. "And it certainly

was powerful."

"Yeah, it got us powerfully stuck in the mud," Kaida said with a laugh.

Rachel could tell that her friends were cranking up for a tiff, so she leaned forward and called out to Stripe, "Will it take very long to get to the Guarded Forest?"

"I've never actually gone that far on the river," Stripe said reluctantly. "We can make it in a few days, I'm sure of that. We'll have to camp a couple of times along the way."

"Camp!" Shaylee yelped. "On the ground? With no tent or sleeping bags or anything?"

"Sure," Stripe said, looking at Shaylee. "I do it all the time. It's not bad, except for the bugs and the monsters, but a fire will keep the bugs away. You'll have to take your chances with the monsters." The little boy giggled at the look of horror on Shaylee's pale face.

"He's just trying to scare you," Kaida said, giving the younger boy a playful shove, but her smile made it clear she wasn't scolding him.

"Looks like he's doing pretty well," Rissa commented as Shaylee practically crawled into her lap. "You don't think they would really have sent us out here if there were monsters, do you?"

"I think they would have done just about anything to get us to restore the Wellspring," Aly said quietly. No one could argue with that. They knew Aly was right.

"Don't you want to know what the monsters look like?" Stripe asked, breaking into their thoughts.

"So we'll recognize them?" Kaida asked with a laugh.

"Don't laugh," Stripe scolded, suddenly serious. "They hate to be laughed at."

"I think it's *you* who doesn't like to be laughed at," Rissa teased.

"Nah," Stripe said. "It's the monsters. You'd not laugh if you saw them. They have eyes as big as my whole head, and they could eat you up with one bite."

"Oh, really?" Kaida asked skeptically.

"You don't believe me," Stripe sulked.

"No so much," Kaida replied.

"I've got proof," Stripe insisted. "You paddle and I'll show you." He dug around in the rucksack he'd brought along. Finally, he pulled out what looked like a thin, oval-shaped, metal plate. Pointedly ignoring Kaida's outstretched hand, he gave it to Aly instead. "It's a scale from one of the monsters. I found it washed up on the riverbank"

"It looks man-made to me," Kaida commented.

"No," Aly said slowly. "I can feel a slight life energy left in it. It came from something alive."

Rachel felt an icy chill at Aly's words, and she noticed that Shaylee shuddered too.

"Let me see," Marisol said eagerly. She took the scale from Aly's hand and smiled at it. "It's gorgeous." She turned it over and over. "Look at it shine in the light. It has so many colors."

When Marisol held it in the light, it did look a bit like a butterfly scale, casting off different colors. Even so, Rachel wasn't sure she would have picked "gorgeous" to describe it. "I just hope we don't run into the creature that belongs to it," Rachel said.

"I think that would be wonderful!" Marisol declared. She turned back toward the river and, holding the scale with both hands, plunged it into the water. Then she sang out, "Come and visit with us!"

"Hey, don't lose that," Stripe protested, grabbing at Marisol's arm.

"Don't rock the boat!" Kaida scolded. The boat was tipping, but Rachel couldn't imagine how either Marisol or Stripe could be tipping it so much. Shaylee shrieked and clung to Rissa as the boat lurched more violently.

Stripe pointed to the water, his eyes wide. "Monster!" he screamed.

A huge head burst from the water in front of the boat as all the girls screamed. The beast looked like a dragon, with a long, toothy snout and seaweed hanging from its chin like a beard. When it poked its head toward the prow of the boat, Rachel saw a flash of scales and realized that they must be resting on the monster's back.

Then Marisol shouted, "Yes! I am coming!" and dove over the side, into the water. The sudden shift in balance was more than the boat could bear, and it capsized, dumping them all into the water.

As Rachel's head slipped under the surface, she remembered Shaylee's earlier panicked cries. Her friend couldn't swim!

CHAPTER 7:
The Princess of the Living Waters

Rachel coughed as her head broke through the silt-filled water. The long gown the Mud Shapers had given her felt like a weight trying to drag her under again. She looked around frantically. "Shaylee! Aly!"

Aly's head popped up next to Rachel. "Are you OK?" she sputtered, pushing her sodden hair out of her face.

"We have to find Shaylee *now!*" Rachel yelled. "She can't swim!"

The girls looked around frantically. They saw Kaida's head break the water closer to the riverbank, with Stripe next to her. Then Rachel saw Shaylee's blond head pop up for a second a little further downstream. Almost instantly, her head disappeared as she flailed her pale hands, splashing frantically in obvious panic.

"Downstream!" Rachel yelled to her sister. She began swimming toward Shaylee with strong strokes, suddenly grateful for all the summers their mother had insisted on swimming lessons. The clinging gown made it hard to kick, but with the river's current pushing her, she quickly reached the spot where Shaylee had appeared. Rachel looked around again. "I can't see through this water!" she yelled. "Can you see her, Aly?"

Aly peered into the gloomy flow. "I see her life glow!" She immediately began swimming downstream again and Rachel followed her. Suddenly Aly dove beneath the surface. When she popped back up a few seconds later, her arm was around Shaylee.

Shaylee coughed and squirmed, clearly frightened. "We've got you," Aly calmly said into her ear. "Don't fight me."

Rachel grabbed one of Shaylee's flailing arms and the sisters began swimming for the riverbank, careful to keep Shaylee's head above water. With the heavy weight of their dresses tugging at them relentlessly, the girls tired quickly, and their strokes slowed. Rachel suddenly felt a cold stab of fear. What if they all drowned within a few feet of shore? Then she heard splashing. Kaida was swimming out to help them.

"You OK?" Kaida said.

"Tired," Rachel gasped. "Can you take Shaylee?"

Kaida wrapped an arm around the smaller girl. "Will you two be OK?"

"I'm OK now," Aly said. The sisters slowly swam to the shallow water next to the riverbank.

"Where are Rissa and Marisol?" Rachel asked, staggering a bit in the shallow water.

"Rissa's on shore with Stripe," Kaida said as she hauled Shaylee onto the sandy bank at the river's edge. "But we haven't seen Marisol."

Rissa ran down to meet them and slipped under Shaylee's arm on one side. She helped Kaida half-carry the younger girl to a dry log. "Are you OK, Shaylee?" Rissa asked anxiously.

Shaylee nodded, still coughing up river water onto the ground near her feet.

Though nearly exhausted from towing Shaylee in, Rachel anxiously turned back toward the water. "We have to find Marisol!"

"She's an excellent swimmer," Aly said. "I would have thought she would beat all of us back to shore."

"Unless the boat hit her on the head," Rissa suggested, "or her gown got caught on something—these things are not exactly made for swimming."

"Can you spot her life energy like you did with Shaylee?" Rachel asked Aly.

"Not from here," her sister said, looking nervously over the water.

"Shaylee was swept downstream," Rachel said. "Maybe we should follow the riverbank downstream and look for Marisol."

"Maybe you'll find my boat, too." Stripe said grumpily. He was huddled in the sand next to Shaylee, though well away from the wet spot marking Shaylee's upset stomach.

66

"Some of us should stay here with Shaylee and Stripe and try to set up camp," Rissa said. "It's going to be dark soon, and it doesn't look like we're going any farther today. We need a fire before Shaylee freezes to death, and some way to get out of the cold wind before it gets dark."

"OK," Kaida said. "Since Aly can talk to plants, she might be helpful with camp. Why don't Rachel and I look for Marisol?"

"And my boat!" Stripe yelled.

Rachel nodded, gave her sister a quick hug, and headed downstream. It was slow going as they carefully picked their way through the roots of the trees and the underbrush. At first they didn't talk, and the silence was broken only by the sounds of hungry insects buzzing and the girls' hands slapping at them.

"I think the river made Marisol crazy somehow," Rachel said finally. "It almost seemed like she called that monster, and she definitely jumped in on purpose."

"We can ask her when we find her," Kaida said. "I know I have a few things to say to her."

"Like what?" The voice came from the river. The girls turned sharply and saw Marisol treading water not far from the bank. She was smiling brightly and somehow had managed to avoid getting her hair plastered to her head with the silt-filled water. In fact, as Rachel moved closer to look, she spotted shells woven into Marisol's hair.

"What are you doing?" Rachel demanded. "You had us worried half to death!" She closed her mouth with a snap, suddenly aware that she sounded just like her mother.

"Don't worry about me." Marisol spoke in an odd rhythm, almost as if she were singing the words. "Water can't hurt me."

"Well, it almost drowned Shaylee," Kaida snapped. "And Stripe's not exactly a great swimmer either."

"Yes, I'm sorry about that," Marisol sang sadly. Then her voice brightened. "But you saved them all!"

"Marisol," Rachel said, "the river is doing weird stuff to you. You're not acting like yourself at all!"

Marisol laughed merrily. "This is exactly like me—the *real* me!"

As Rachel took a step toward the water, her foot slipped on the bank, nearly pitching her into the river. "Look, just get out of there. We need to find Stripe's boat and figure out how we're going to get dry again."

Marisol frowned slightly. "I can't come out, but I would be glad to help find Stripe's boat!"

"What do you mean, you can't get out?" Kaida asked. "Just swim over here and climb out. We'll help you."

"You don't understand," Marisol said. "I will show you." She leaned back in the water as if to begin a backstroke and lifted what should have been her feet from the water. But they weren't feet. She had a tail. A scaly tail with a broad, flat flipper at the end. Marisol laughed cheerily at their shocked expressions. "I'm a mermaid! Isn't it wonderful? I've *always*, always wanted to be a mermaid!"

Rachel just shook her head numbly. A *mermaid*. What were they going to do now?

Suddenly the water just beyond Marisol began to

churn. The huge head of the river monster burst into the air, water streaming from the weedy fins on the sides of its head. As its head dipped toward Marisol, Rachel screamed, "Marisol, look out! Behind you!"

CHAPTER 8:
Full of Surprises

Kaida scooped up a rock on the riverbank and threw it hard toward the monster's face. "Duck, Marisol!" she shouted as she bent for another rock.

But Marisol raised her hand, and, as if at her bidding, a wave rose up from the river to slap the rock away before it could hit the dragon's face. Then Marisol's laughter rang out across the water. "Don't be scared. The river dragons won't hurt me. They wouldn't hurt anyone." The huge head bent low and Marisol patted the end of his snout.

"That thing tried to drown all of us!" Kaida shouted. "It isn't some kind of puppy, Marisol!"

"He only wanted us to come into the water and play," Marisol said. "Especially me. He didn't know we ... well, you ... might drown."

"It's dangerous!" Kaida insisted.

"No, it's not!" Marisol said, just as firmly. "Don't you recognize him? He's the river dragon from my key. I was *supposed* to meet the river dragons—it's my destiny!"

"So you can *talk* to those things?" Rachel asked. As Marisol patted it, he river dragon seemed to wriggle with pleasure. Rachel had to admit that it didn't exactly look vicious, but it sure was big.

"Not exactly," Marisol said. "River dragons don't think in words like we do—just in feelings and pictures. I can share their thoughts and send them mine."

"Do you think it could find Stripe's boat for us?" Kaida asked.

"He could do more than that," Marisol said proudly. "They're very fast. He could tow the boat for us. I think we could reach the Guarded Forest sometime tomorrow. When I pictured the bear Guardians in my thoughts, I got the feeling it wouldn't take long to reach them."

"Could we just go now?" Kaida asked.

Rachel looked around and shivered. The gloom over the water was deepening. It would be fully dark soon, and she really wanted to dry out and get warm. "I think it might be better to wait until morning. But we need that boat."

Marisol nodded and turned toward the dragon. She leaned close to it and, in a moment, the dragon had turned and flung himself downstream. Just before he disappeared under the water, his tail broke the surface and slapped it, sending a cold wash over Rachel and Kaida.

"I think I could really hate those things," Kaida grumbled, wiping water from her face and arms.

"We need to get back to the others," Rachel said. "Can you swim up to where we left them?"

"I can swim anywhere!" Marisol said happily. She turned and, with a flip of her tail, raced upstream at an amazing speed.

"Wow!" Kaida said. "I bet the swim team would love her in this condition!"

"I'm sure there's something in the rule book about tails. I just hope the Guardians have some good ideas on how to turn her back into our regular Marisol again." Rachel turned and began pushing back through the underbrush. As she stomped and squished, she was suddenly struck by a thought that made her laugh.

"What?" Kaida asked as she paused to pluck a briar from the trailing hem of her skirt.

"I just remembered how much I liked pretending to be a princess when I was little," Rachel said. "But I don't remember ever imagining this much squishy stuff, and I know I *never* imagined these bugs. My princess phase was more about tea parties and tiaras."

Kaida laughed. "What's a tea party without mud, muck and bloodsuckers? I never played princess. I was too busy playing Olympic athlete and gold medalist—my family is kind of *into* sports."

"Oh, really?" Rachel teased. "I hadn't noticed."

"Hey, I'm not *all* about the sports, though—I really like to cook, too."

"I didn't know that," Rachel said. Then she yelped and stopped while Kaida helped her untangle her hair from a hanging branch. "You know—ouch!—Aly likes to cook, too. Maybe you guys can get together and make a roots and berries soup for supper. Ouch!"

"Yum," Kaida said, pulling the last strand of hair loose. She slapped at something flying around her head. "Maybe I'll throw in some buzzing bugs for protein."

"Who says princesses can't live off the land?"

Finally, the girls broke through to the clearing. They arrived to find their friends dragging ferns into what looked like a vine igloo. "How did you make that?" Kaida asked, clearly impressed.

"It made itself," Rissa said, "with a little help from Aly, the Plant Princess." Then she frowned. "You guys couldn't find Marisol?"

"No, we found her," Rachel said. "I thought she would get here a long time before us."

"I did," a voice called from the water. "I just waited for you down here."

"Marisol!" Shaylee rushed to the edge of the water. The other girls followed, but in the gloom, they could barely see their friend.

"Why are you still in the water?" Rissa asked. "Are you all right?"

"I'm terrific!" Marisol sang out. "And look what my new friend found." She gestured downstream and the group turned to see Stripe's boat slowly moving toward them.

"My boat!" Stripe yelled. "Who's driving my boat?" Just

then, the boat drew close enough so that they could see the scaly creature that was nudging it along. "Monster!"

"River dragon," Marisol corrected him primly. "And my friend."

"You still haven't told us why you're in the water," Rissa said, folding her arms and tapping her foot impatiently.

Marisol, Rachel and Kaida explained Marisol's scaly transformation from girl to mermaid. "I wish I could see your tail," Shaylee said. "Is it beautiful like the tails of the mermaids in the movies?"

"It's gorgeous," Marisol said. "And you should see the fantastic stuff the river dragons are finding for me! You could make jewelry for a year out of these shells and pearls and even gems. The colors are awesome!"

"Right now, we need to make a fire before we freeze to death in these wet clothes," Rissa interrupted. "And we need food—all Stripe could find were some berries he said were safe to eat, but it's certainly not enough to fill us up."

"Oh, right—I forgot that you must be cold. I don't seem to get cold anymore," Marisol said. She paused, then added, "The river dragons don't make fire, but they could catch some fish."

"Can you make a fire?" Rachel asked Stripe.

"Of course," Stripe said. "I have been building fires since I was a baby. But my fire kit was in my bag, and I lost that when we fell into the river."

"Can the river dragons find it?" Rachel asked Marisol.

"It wouldn't help. It would be ruined by the water."

"You know, I've been camping lots of times," Kaida said. "All you need for a fire is a spark and dry tinder. I'll give it a try."

"Here, I found some dry lichen," Stripe said. "It burns easily."

"We'll finish filling the vine tent with ferns for sleeping while you do the fire thing," Rissa said, turning to go back to the shelter. Aly and Shaylee followed her.

"I'll help with the fire," Rachel said.

"And I will stay here and get the fish from the monsters," Stripe said.

"River dragons!" Marisol's voice carried across the water, but it had grown too dark to see her.

Rachel shivered as she arranged a circle of rocks on bare dirt to contain the fire they hoped to start. She laid small dry sticks carefully, leaving room between them for air—she knew it was important that a fire get air. "So how are you going to start the fire?" she asked.

"Well, you either need friction or a spark," Kaida said. "For a spark, you need the right kind of rocks."

"Do we have the right kind?" Rachel could barely see the rocks, and she had no idea what kind they were—except that they were hard.

Kaida sighed. "I don't know. I guess we bang them and see if they spark." She began banging rocks together while Rachel watched closely for any sign of a spark. At one point, Kaida nearly caught the end of her friend's nose between the rocks she was banging. Rachel didn't watch quite so closely after that.

Finally, Kaida had tried all the rocks they had. "I didn't see any sparks," she said.

"Me either."

"So, it's time to try friction," Kaida said. "It's like rubbing your hands together to make them warm. Only you rub sticks together hard enough to make a fire."

Rachel didn't think that sounded very likely, but she sat quietly as Kaida found a dry stick with a deep indentation where a smaller branch had broken off it, leaving a thin crack. Then Kaida put the pointed end of another stick into that crack. Bracing the bigger stick between her knees, she began to twirl the thin stick back and forth, back and forth, between her palms.

Long after Rachel would have given up, Kaida kept spinning the pointed stick.

Eventually the other girls finished arranging the bedding and joined Rachel and Kaida. They all sat silently while Kaida focused persistently on the sticks. The night air was getting cooler and Rachel shivered in her sodden clothes.

"I have the fish!" Stripe called. As he walked up to the group, they could see that he had turned up his shirtfront to form a basket, and it was loaded with small fish. "The water princess says she will be sleeping in the river tonight," he said. The other girls shuddered slightly at the thought. The night air was cold enough; the river must be freezing!

Stripe stood over Kaida and Rachel. "I'll need firelight to clean these fish."

"I'm working on it," Kaida muttered through tightly clenched teeth.

"What are you going to use to clean all those fish?" Rissa asked.

Holding his shirtfront with one hand, Stripe reached down with the other to lift one pant leg and pull a short knife from its sheath. "This!"

"You have a knife!" Rissa crowed. "Let me see that."

Stripe passed it over reluctantly and Rissa used the sharp blade to cut off the bottom of her dress until it was little longer than knee length. "Now I won't be tripping over the dratted thing anymore."

"Do mine, please," Aly asked, and Rissa soon had her skirt shortened.

"So you want me to do yours?" she asked Shaylee.

The smaller girl shook her head. "No, I don't want to ruin the dress."

"I think the river already did that," Rissa said, then turned to Rachel. "Want me to do you?"

Rachel had been hunched close to Kaida, ready to feed dry lichen at the first hint of smoke. "Do you think I have time?" she asked her friend.

"I think you have all night," Kaida said, throwing the sticks across the clearing in frustration. "I tried everything I could think of. I don't know what to do."

"We need a fire," Stripe snapped.

"I know we need a fire!" Kaida yelled. "What do you think I've been doing right here?" She pointed toward the neatly stacked twigs. As her voice rose to a shout, the tiny pile of sticks suddenly burst into flame. All the girls leapt back.

"Wow," Shaylee said. "I think you made a fire."

Rachel recovered enough to begin piling more sticks on the fire before it could burn out. While Stripe set to cleaning the fish and the other girls gathered sticks for holding the fish over the fire, Kaida sat very still, staring into the flames.

"Are you OK?" Rachel asked.

"I made a fire," Kaida said, then she grinned. "I am Super Camper!"

"I think we'll be more comfortable without the gowns." Rissa stood up and shucked off her gown, leaving on the long linen camisole and underskirt. "If we hang the dresses on the branches, they should dry more quickly."

Soon all the girls had stripped down and hung their gowns in the tree branches. They huddled around the fire, roasting the small fish and snacking on sweet berries. "It's starting to feel like real camping," Kaida said.

"Thanks to you," Rachel said.

Shaylee looked out into the darkness in the direction of the river. "Do you think Marisol will be OK?"

"She should be," Rissa said. "She's got the world's biggest guard dog."

"Do you think we'll be able to change her back?"

"I don't know," Rissa admitted. "Maybe I should have tried a spell."

"Not a good idea," Kaida said. "She would have ended up as *all* tuna instead of just half."

Rachel could feel another argument coming on, so she said the first thing that popped into her head. "I wonder what our families are doing."

"Freaking out completely," Kaida said. "By now, they must know we're not in the clubhouse."

"They've probably called the police," Shaylee said.

"My dad *is* the police," Rissa said. She and her dad had moved from Washington D.C. to Portal so that he could take a job as chief of police. "He worried so much about me growing up in a city. He must be totally panicked over this."

"I hope my mom isn't crying," Shaylee said. At that, all the girls fell silent, thinking about their moms. Rachel felt tears sting her eyes. Were they ever going to see their families again?

Kaida cleared her throat. "Well, this isn't helping anything," she said. "We need to get some sleep so we can finish our mission tomorrow and go home. We've gotten this far. I just *know* we'll get home." She stood and scooped up a handful of sand to begin putting the fire out.

"Don't do that," Stripe said. "I'll stay out here and watch it." He wrinkled his nose as he looked at the vine hut. "It's a little small in there."

The girls crawled into the vine hut. They all huddled together while Aly focused her powers on the vines that formed the hut. The girls watched as the vines slowly wove together to close the opening and keep out the cold. Snuggled close together for warmth and comfort, they began to drift off.

Just before she fell asleep, Rachel thought of Kaida's confident words about getting home. She certainly hoped her friend was right.

CHAPTER 9:
Speed Boat

Rachel woke up as the soft morning light crept into the vine hut. She sat up and stretched, then watched as the vines began unweaving themselves and withdrawing into the forest. "Being woven like that isn't really good for them," Aly said softly near Rachel's ear. "I don't want to leave them that way."

"Maybe you could get the vine wall at the Guarded Forest to do that," Rachel said.

Aly shrugged. "Maybe, but I sensed strong purpose there, as if the vines know they must protect the spring. I'm not sure they would undo the wall for me."

"Probably not," Rissa said. "Nothing here is easy."

The girls crawled out of the hut and saw that the fire was out. Stripe had poured sand over it and stirred the ashes. "I guess he is a good camper," Kaida said.

"I know I'm glad I didn't have to clean the fish," Rissa said. "I totally did not want to deal with fish guts."

"Eeuuww!" Shaylee shuddered delicately. "Can we not talk about that? I ate some of those fish."

"Yeah," Rissa said, "but you didn't have to eat the guts."

"Eeuuww!"

"Well, I wouldn't mind a little fish right now," Kaida said. "I'm hungry."

"There's no time for fishing," Stripe said as he raced toward them from the river. "I want to get going before those monsters decide to take off with my boat."

"I don't think they'd do that," Aly said.

"You never can tell with monsters."

With no breakfast to eat, the group had no reason to linger at the camp, so the girls slipped their tattered gowns back on for warmth and trooped down to the river. Walking behind Rissa, Rachel noticed that between their mud bath and their dip in the river, all the temporary color was gone from Rissa's hair. "Rissa," Rachel said in surprise, "your hair is a really pretty color!"

Rissa put a hand to her cropped strawberry blond hair. "You think so?" Then she laughed. "Don't get used to it. When we get home, I'm planning on a pink period in Shaylee's honor."

As they scrambled into the boat, the girls looked nervously at the river dragon, which was waiting patiently near the bow of the boat. But "patiently" for a river dragon included occasional twitches and wiggles that set the boat bobbing like a cork.

"Where's Marisol?" Kaida asked as she climbed in to sit beside Stripe. The girls called their friend's name for several minutes before Marisol's dark head popped up above the water. Her hair was woven with even more shells and pearls.

"Guess what?" she asked. Then, without waiting for an answer, she said, "The river dragons told me there are more mer-people. Lots of them! We just have to head downstream to the sea." She pointed downstream.

"Marisol," Aly said gently, "that's the wrong direction. We need to reach the Guarded Forest."

"Well, I know that," their friend said sulkily. "I just thought it was cool. You know, more people like me. I mean, the river dragons are fun, but they can't really talk."

"We can talk," Kaida said. "And we'll be happy to chat with you as we head for the Guarded Forest."

"All right, all right," Marisol said. Then she ducked under the surface and swam up to the river dragon. After a moment of mermaid-to-river dragon communicating, she shouted, "He brought the boat this far by bumping it from behind, but I don't think that would feel very good for you onboard. We need some rope!"

"We have this." Rissa had brought the scraps she'd cut off their gowns the night before. "I thought it might come in handy. We'll have to tie it together to make a rope."

Stripe pulled out his knife and sliced the pieces of gown into long strips, which they wove together and tied into a long rope. "It's sure the prettiest rope I've ever seen,"

Shaylee said as they finished. "Look at all the gorgeous colors and lace."

Stripe tied one end of the rope to the front of the boat. Marisol tied a fat knot in the other end and passed it to the dragon. He took it in his mouth and began pulling. When the little boat lurched forward, the girls cheered.

Soon the dragon was racing through the water, pulling the boat so fast that the wind whipped the girls' hair around their faces wildly. Stripe laughed out loud. "I want my boat to do this always!"

"Then you had better make friends with the river dragon," Marisol yelled to him. She held onto one of the dragon's leafy back fins so that he could tow her, too.

"I cannot wait to get home," Stripe said, "and tell everyone how the monster made my boat fly!"

"*River dragon!*" Marisol corrected.

"River dragon," Stripe agreed. "Do you think the river dragon would pull a boat for me again?"

Marisol leaned against the river dragon's neck for a moment, then nodded. "He would like that. He thinks this is a wonderful game. The river dragons love games."

"Like the world's biggest, scaliest puppy," Rissa said.

"Marisol," Shaylee called out, "what's it like being a mermaid?"

"It's incredible!" her friend answered. "The water feels warm, and I can see underwater as clearly as you see me. The fish flash like silver lightning, and there are crabs at the river bottom that do the funniest sideways dance." She smiled dreamily. "But the dragons say the sea is even better.

I could dance with the dolphins."

Rachel frowned. Her friend's love of her new form worried her. Would she be ready to change back when they got to the forest? "Marisol, do the twins know how to swim yet?"

Marisol grinned. She loved talking about the twins her parents had adopted from China. "No, but they love the water too. You should see them splash in the tub. Mom calls them 'the tsunami twins.'"

"Sounds adorable," Rachel said.

"Totally," Marisol agreed. "And when they say my name, Nina calls me 'Mari' and Marco calls me 'Sol,' so I only get my whole name when they're both calling me at the same time. But that happens a lot. Mom says I'm their favorite person in the world." Marisol's smile faded. "I miss them."

"I think we'll get back to them," Kaida said. "I just know it. We're going to get home when this is all over."

Marisol looked ruefully toward her tail. "I hope Mom's ready to buy a really big fish tank."

CHAPTER 10:
A Whale of a Tail

The boat raced up the river as the girls thought about home. Stripe was the only one still wearing a grin as he crouched near the front of the boat with the wind in his face. Suddenly he shouted, "*Stop!*"

The river dragon stopped so abruptly that the boat slammed into the back of his neck. The jolt was enough to knock all the passengers out of their seats. "What did you do that for?" Rissa demanded.

"Look!" Stripe pointed to a low-hanging tree just ahead of them. Its branches were full of dark blue fruit. "Twilight fruit is very good."

"You nearly killed us because you wanted a snack?" Rissa shouted.

Stripe glared. "I didn't get any breakfast!"

"Please don't fight!" Marisol begged. "We can get some fruit and then keep going. The river dragon showed me that we are almost there."

The boat eased up under the fruit tree, and everyone picked a few pieces. It tasted like a cross between a very ripe peach and a plum, and it had large seeds in the center. After taking a few bites, Rissa admitted that Stripe's idea wasn't that bad. "But next time, maybe you could let us ease to a stop."

Stripe just nodded as juice dripped down his chin.

With full tummies, the girls felt much cheerier, and when the dragon brought the boat to full speed again, Stripe wasn't the only one grinning. But as the dragon had promised, they soon slowed and came to a stop near a long, sandy bank. The river dragon dropped the rope, then gently nudged the boat toward the sand. The girls splashed through the shallow water and onto the bank.

"This is the edge of the Guarded Forest," Marisol called from deeper water. "I will wait for you here. I'm not exactly built for overland travel at the moment. Maybe when you restore the magic you can come back and turn me back into a girl."

"I have a different idea," Kaida said. "We haven't even tried the most obvious solution."

"What's that?"

"In the movies, when a girl turns into a mermaid from getting wet, all she has to do to turn back is get dry."

Marisol smiled. "Do you really think it could be as easy as that?"

"It was as easy as that when you turned into a mermaid."

"Let's try it, but I can't get all the way to land. The water is too shallow, and I don't crawl very well."

"We'll get you," Kaida said as she waded back into the water. Marisol swam as close to the riverbank as she could, scooting a bit in the shallows. Rachel and Rissa waded out after Kaida, while Aly stood on the riverbank with Shaylee. The younger girl was still a bit fearful of wading in the river. Half-carrying and half-dragging, the girls got Marisol onto the riverbank and set her down on the sand, well above the water line.

"Now, I guess we wait for you to dry out," Rissa said.

The girls waited, pacing back and forth, while Marisol fidgeted uncomfortably on the dry sand. Finally, when her tail felt completely dry and she still had not changed, they had to admit that the plan did not seem to be working.

"It makes me feel a little sick to be so dry," Marisol said. "Please help me back into the water before you go."

"We're not giving up yet," Kaida said. "Hey, the Mud Shapers said our beads were magic. Maybe you can wish on yours or something. Do you still have it?"

When Marisol drew up her tail, the other girls could see that the leather thong seemed to have magically grown to encircle her tail just above the flipper. The beautiful blue bead lay on the scales. Marisol gripped it in her hand and closed her eyes. "I wish to be a girl again." Nothing happened.

"I could have told you that wouldn't work," Stripe called from the boat. "The beads won't have power again until you Princesses fix the Wellspring. Their power comes from that magic."

"But after we restore that magic, will the bead change her back?" Rachel asked.

Stripe shrugged. "The beads' magic is different for each person, but it's always something you really need."

"I really need to be a girl again before I go home," Marisol said.

"But Princess, you might need something else even more," Stripe replied.

None of the girls could imagine Marisol needing anything more than being a girl again. "I guess you'll have to put me back in the water and go fix the Wellspring," Marisol said sadly.

Rachel shook her head. "Don't you remember? The Guardians said it will take *all* of our magic to restore the spring. We need Marisol with us."

"Well, I can't carry her through the woods," Kaida snapped.

"The bears probably could," Rissa said.

Marisol looked alarmed. "I don't think I can be dry that long. I'm feeling worse and worse."

The girls stood silently around Marisol for a moment. They didn't want to leave her behind. They weren't even sure if they could. But what choice did they have?

Finally, Kaida turned to Rissa. "I think you should try another spell."

Rissa stared at her, open-mouthed. "You want me to try a spell? *You?* Who are you, and what did you do with Kaida?"

"Very funny. Look, we don't have any choice. Just make sure you don't mention 'stuck' or 'blown up' or 'eaten by monsters' in the rhyme, OK?"

Rissa sniffed and turned to Marisol. "You want me to try a spell on you, to turn you back into a girl?"

"Yes," Marisol said. "I'm ready to be me again—really, *really* ready."

Rissa nodded and looked at the others. "I think we all need to agree. Does everyone want me to try this?"

"We don't have a lot of other choices," Aly said softly. "I believe you can do it."

"OK." Rissa closed her eyes. The other girls joined hands around her and Marisol. Rissa cleared her throat and began. "Water Princess back on land no longer needs her tail. Change back to legs and skin and clothes. Magic rhyme, don't fail."

The girls held their breath as seconds passed without a change. Then Marisol's tail began to sparkle and shimmer. The scales and fins seemed to dissolve, revealing her legs and feet. Then the gown Marisol had been wearing flowed down from the remnant that had been her shirt when she was a mermaid. Before their eyes, she was completely transformed back to herself—legs, gown, slippers and all!

Marisol jumped to her feet and threw her arms around Rissa. "You did it! Thank you, thank you, thank you!"

The girls hugged each other, jumping up and down. Shaylee even ran back and tried to hug Stripe, but the younger boy wasn't having any of that. "Don't you think you should go restore the Wellspring?" he finally asked.

"Yeah," Kaida said. She pointed to the dark woods that edged the sandy riverbank. "Are you sure that's the Guarded Forest?"

Stripe looked toward the gloomy woods. "I'm sure."

"Can you lead us to the Wellspring?"

"No!" Stripe folded his arms. "I don't know where it is, and I'm not going in there at all. I did my job and now I want to go home."

Marisol shrugged. "I guess that's fair. Do you want the river dragon to tow you home in your boat?"

Stripes eyes lit up. "All the way back so everyone can see? Yes!"

As the girls laughed, Marisol walked to the edge of the river. Taking care not to get her feet wet, she exchanged thoughts with the river dragon. "He's happy to go with you, Stripe."

"Great!" the boy said. Then he looked sad. "Will you Princesses come back to see me and the other Folk again sometime?"

"I don't know," Rachel said. "Maybe not."

The boy nodded glumly. "I will remember you always."

"And I can't imagine *ever* forgetting you," Rissa said.

The girls all hugged the protesting boy. He voiced his protest, though Rachel noticed that he didn't squirm away. Finally, they backed away from Stripe's boat and watched as the river dragon pulled it out into the water. Stripe and the girls waved wildly to each other until the boat was out of sight.

When Stripe had disappeared downstream, the ragged group turned toward the tree line. "I don't suppose anyone has any magical sense of the right way to go?" Kaida asked. All the girls shook their heads.

"I'm not sure it matters," Rachel said. "I suspect the Guardians will find us quickly enough after we get in the woods. I just hope they aren't too mad about how long we've taken to get here." The girls pictured the huge bears angry and shivered.

CHAPTER 11:
A Walk in the Woods

"Is it just me, or is there something seriously creepy about these woods?" Rissa asked. By now the girls were deep enough into the trees that they had lost sight of the river. "I mean, the woods feel way creepier than the first time we were in them."

"The life force in here is ... strange," Aly said, looking around. "When we were here before, it was brighter. Now the life force of the trees is like those around the Mud Shaper's village—something is twisting them. It all feels ... wrong."

Rachel pointed to a sapling whose trunk was nearly as twisted as a vine. "The trees look like they're sick or something."

Aly walked to the twisted tree and laid her hand gently

on its bark. "It doesn't have any kind of disease, I don't think." She chewed her lip quietly. "They almost look like the plants I saw in that exhibit at the science fair, where someone proved how plant stems will twist and turn to find the light."

"They're looking for light?" Rissa looked up. "It's not really that dark in here."

Aly shook her head. "Not light, exactly."

"They are looking for life." It was the rumbling voice of Fleet speaking in Rachel's head. She yelped in surprise, then turned to see the huge bear behind them. "All life in this forest comes from the Wellspring," Fleet continued. "In their own way, the trees are looking for the Wellspring, too, just as you are, and they are doing just about as well."

"How did you sneak up on us?" Rachel asked.

"You princesses make a great deal of noise when you walk," Fleet said.

Shaylee edged closer to Rachel. "Is he mad at us?" she squeaked.

The bear tilted his head to look at the tiny blonde. "Why would I be angry with you?"

Rachel tried for a nonchalant shrug. "We haven't fixed the Wellspring."

"I know." The bear nodded.

"We figured you probably wanted it fixed by now."

The bear blinked. "Have you not done your best to face each challenge? Why would any of the Guardians be angry with you?"

"He's not mad," Rachel told the other girls. Then she turned back to Fleet. "Um, as you probably noticed, we're not exactly sure where the Wellspring is."

"I suspected that when I saw you were walking in a circle." Fleet responded.

Rachel thought she detected a hint of sarcasm from the bear, but she decided to ignore it. "Could you show us the right direction?" she asked.

Fleet nodded. "I am afraid you must walk. I cannot carry you all, and the other Guardians are ... ill."

"What happened to them?" Rachel asked.

"What happened to who?" Shaylee asked, tugging on Rachel's arm. Rachel repeated Fleet's words quickly, still looking at the great bear.

"Our life comes directly from the Wellspring," Fleet said quietly. "We lost our magical abilities some time ago. Now our life here is running out."

"None of the Guardians have ... died, have they?" Rachel asked.

"Not yet." The bear turned to push into the woods. "Come, please."

As they followed Fleet, Rachel quietly told the other girls about the Guardians. For the first time since Rachel had met her, Rissa looked totally deflated.

"It's my fault," the girl mumbled. "Me and my stupid spell. We lost all that time!"

"She must not blame herself," Fleet said. "Tell her, Princess, there is no blame here."

"I've got it covered," Rachel said, then she laid her

hand on Rissa's arm. "Your spells aren't stupid and neither are you. We're all trying to work without directions here."

"And don't forget," Marisol said, "if you hadn't tried a spell, I would still be in the river."

Rissa nodded but still looked sad as they pushed through increasingly dense underbrush. Prickly thorns caught at their ragged gowns, tearing at the sleeves and skirts. When the group had to pause to untangle Shaylee from a particularly sticky thorn, the younger girl sighed. "This was such a pretty dress. I'm starting to look more and more like Cinderella before the fairy godmother."

"Walk as close behind me as you can," Fleet said. "It should help."

When Rachel passed the direction on, Shaylee wrinkled her nose. "What if he poops or something? I mean, he is a an animal, after all."

"I have not eaten lately. I believe you should be safe," Fleet assured them. Rachel repeated his message, though she suspected he was being sarcastic again.

"Why haven't you eaten lately?" Kaida asked suddenly.

Rachel passed on Fleet's answer. "The trees of the Guarded Forest have not flowered nor borne fruit for some time. Again, it will be better when Wellspring's magic is restored."

"So everything is dying?" Rachel asked. "Then why do there seem to be more of these briars?"

"You did not notice them so much when we carried you. And, as some life feels the magic fading, it reaches for a darker force." The bear's voice sounded hesitant. "It is difficult for me to explain, but not everything in the forest can be trusted."

Rachel shivered.

Suddenly they heard a tremendous bellow coming from deeper in the forest.

"Honeyglow!" Fleet roared, turning toward the sound and crashing through the brush.

CHAPTER 12:
Dark Magic

"Fleet!" Rachel yelled after him. "What is it?" But the bear didn't answer.

"What is it?" Kaida asked.

"I don't know," Rachel said. "But we'd better hurry up and follow him."

The girls raced through the broken brush, scrambling over small trees that Fleet had knocked down in his wake. They soon lost sight of the great bear, though they paused only when a branch or briar caught at them. However, they had no trouble following the sound of Honeyglow's frantic roars.

Finally, the girls burst into a small clearing, where two huge boulders stood so closely together, it was as though they were one. Honeyglow stood beside the boulders, slightly hunched on her hind feet and leaning toward the rocks. Her head was twisted awkwardly, as if she were trying to press the side of her face deep into the stone. Her front paws twitched, digging at the air.

Fleet stood on his hind feet as well, facing Honeyglow, and using one front leg to push himself slightly away from the boulder. He bent over Honeyglow, his muzzle thrust deep into the fur at her neck as if he intended to rip out her throat.

"Fleet!" Rachel shouted. "What's wrong?"

"There is a vine wrapped around Honeyglow's neck!" Fleet thought at her, his jaws still biting at the smaller bear's throat. "It's a parasite created by dark magic." Honeyglow jerked her head away from the rock and bellowed again in pain and fear. Fleet threw his weight against her, pressing her back against the rocks so she had to stop struggling. He growled in frustration "The vine is working its way through her fur. If it reaches her skin, it will feed off her blood. Already it is too deep for me to reach with my teeth."

"A blood-sucking plant?" Rachel cried. "Can we help you?"

"My paws are too big to reach between the boulders," Fleet said, panting as he held the smaller bear still. "Crawl between us and reach into the crack. It is wider near the ground. Puncture the sac that grows at the base of the stem. When you do that, the vine will release her." The huge bear bit down on one of his long, thick claws, breaking it off close to the paw. "You can cut into it with this."

Rachel shakily took the razor-sharp claw and dropped

to her knees. She squeezed between the bears, ducking once when Honeyglow's flailing front paws nearly raked across her skull. She crawled forward until she reached the rocks and tried to shove her arm into the space between them, but the gap was too narrow to reach past the middle of her forearm. When she tried to force her arm in farther, a hair-thin vine whipped out and slapped across her wrist, slicing through the thick sleeve of her gown. Rachel jerked her arm back, raking scratches along her wrist and hand as she pulled it from between the rough rocks.

"My arm won't fit," she said.

Honeyglow moaned and the bigger bear growled again. "We must find something that will fit."

"I can try," Aly said. "Tell me what to do."

"Your arm isn't any thinner than mine," Rachel argued. "We have to reach in and puncture a sac at the bottom of the vine to make it let go of Honeyglow."

"It's a plant," Aly said, kneeling next to her sister. "Maybe I can talk to it."

"It won't listen," Fleet said. "It draws life from the Darker Source. You are not its Princess."

"Fleet says it won't work," Rachel said. "We have to get into that crack somehow."

Then they heard a small, shaky voice. "I can try."

The girls turned to see Shaylee near tears. She was the smallest of the girls and her arms were much thinner than those of anyone else. She was also clearly terrified.

"You have to be quick," Rachel said. "The vines will fight back."

Shaylee was trembling, but she nodded and dropped to her knees, squirming between the bears until she reached the crack. Fleet shifted position to give her more room, and Rachel pushed in as well as she could to watch and murmur encouragement to Shaylee.

She saw the slender girl take a deep, shuddering breath and thrust her arm into the crack. The space was tight but she pushed and wiggled, reaching deeper and deeper. Another small vine slipped out and waved in the air, feeling for something to grab.

"Watch out for the vine!" Rachel yelled.

Shaylee turned her face sharply away from the waving vine's reach and it tangled harmlessly in a lock of hair. Shaylee winced when the small vine pulled her hair, but she kept pushing her arm deeper into the crack until she felt a spongy mass. "This is so gross," she said as she tore through the mass with Fleet's sharp claw. Wet goo covered her hand. "Oh, gross, gross, *gross!*"

She felt the bears shift beside her. "You did it!" Rachel yelled. "Shaylee, you did it!" Shaylee pulled her arm free and grinned as her friends hauled her to her feet and engulfed her in a hug.

Honeyglow shook off the dead bits of vine still clinging to her fur. She bowed low before Shaylee.

"She wants to give you a ride the rest of the way to the Wellspring," Rachel said, grinning.

Shaylee was scrubbing the goo from her hand with a ragged piece of skirt. She straightened up and smiled at the bear. "Is she sure she doesn't need to rest or something?"

"Probably," Rachel said. "But she insists, and you don't weigh much."

The girls helped boost Shaylee onto Honeyglow's back, and then they all turned back toward the Wellspring.

"So, do you think we might run into more killer plants?" Rachel asked.

"It is unlikely," Fleet answered after a long pause. "They are still few—for now."

"'Unlikely' isn't the same as impossible," Rachel said. "I really don't like killer plants."

The bear nudged her reassuringly, nearly knocking Rachel into a thicket. "Do not be afraid, Princess. We are almost there."

Finally, they reached the clearing that bordered the tall tangled wall of vines. "They still look healthy," Kaida said glumly. "I don't suppose Fleet has actual suggestions this time for getting us in there?"

"It is still a task only you can do," Fleet answered.

"No," Rachel told Kaida. "But we have our secret weapon this time—Aly the vine whisperer!" She grinned at her sister, but Aly only stared at the wall thoughtfully as she walked toward it.

The other girls followed her as she moved closer to the wall. "What if it isn't in the mood to listen?" Kaida said. "Those killer plants weren't exactly chatty."

"The plants in this wall are totally different," Rachel said. "Right, Fleet?"

The great bear didn't answer. "Fleet?" Rachel said, turning around. The bears were gone.

"I guess bears aren't big on goodbyes," Rissa said with a frown.

"I guess," Rachel said. She knew the bears weren't supposed to help, but somehow she felt a lot safer in their big, shaggy company. She sighed and turned back to the wall. "I guess it's Princess time."

CHAPTER 13:
Restoring the Magic

"Oh, goodie," Rissa said. "We're back where we started. Anybody want to dance?"

"Well, fun as that sounds, I vote Aly does the plant whisperer thing on the vines," Kaida said. "Can you tell them to go away?"

"I can try." Aly stepped closer to the vines, resting her head against the thick wall. Everyone else waited silently. After a few moments, Aly shook her head. "They won't go away and leave the Wellspring unprotected—not until the magic is restored. I sense that they are troubled by the Darker Source that Fleet talked about."

"But we can't restore the Wellspring if they won't go away," Rachel said, her voice rising in frustration. "Can you ask them again? Maybe picture how happy everyone will be when they get out of the way and let us fix the magic thing?"

While Aly leaned against the wall again, Kaida said, "Well, I don't want to wait around until these vines go renegade blood sucker or something. We've tried being reasonable. Now I'm going to try a more direct route." She walked back and forth next to the wall, examining and shaking vines. They moved only slightly when she heaved against them.

Kaida took a deep breath and started to climb. "This isn't too hard," she called down. "It's a little like rock climbing, but there are more places to hold onto." Rachel knew Kaida often went rock climbing with her dad.

"Come on—it's easy!" Kaida shouted. "We'll just climb over the vine wall!"

Shaylee stepped up to the wall and pushed up her sleeves. "I don't mind trying. The sooner we get over the wall, the sooner we get home." She hiked up the ragged edge of her gown and used her jeweled belt to hold it. Then she grabbed a vine and began to climb.

Soon everyone but Aly was up in the vines. Rachel was surprised at how easy they were to climb. The vines were neatly woven together in a mat that offered thousands of hand and footholds.

Suddenly Kaida yelled at them from above. At almost the same instant, Rachel felt a vine snake out and wrap tightly around her wrist. Another snared her ankle and then another thicker vine whipped around her waist. In seconds she was stuck fast. She looked around and saw

Rissa beside her, struggling in the same viney grip. "Help!" she yelled.

From far below, Rachel heard Aly's voice say, "Don't struggle. You could fall."

Rachel twisted and looked down. Aly was still on the ground. She had not tried to climb the vines.

"I'll try to get the vines to let you go," Aly yelled. "Hold still and don't fight the vines! I think I'm getting through to them about why we're here."

"Then why are they still trying to squeeze us to death?" Kaida yelled.

"Hush—give her a chance." Rachel's neck ached from the awkward position but she kept her eyes on her sister. Aly laid her hand on the thick vines at the base of the living wall. Rachel held her breath, hoping the vines didn't snare her sister, too. When she saw movement around Aly, she screamed, "Watch out, the vines are moving!"

Hundreds of thin vines snaked out from the wall and wrapped around Aly. They didn't twist tightly like the vines on Rachel's arms and legs, but wove together until Aly had vanished completely, as if she had become a part of the wall itself. "Aly!" Rachel screamed again, thrashing hard against the vines that gripped her wrists and ankles.

Then more of the tiny thin vines shot out around Rachel, weaving a capsule around her just as they had around Aly. Rachel struggled but the capsule was woven tightly. The thick vines around her arms and legs slipped away and Rachel felt movement beneath her as vines opened up.

Soon she was sliding down as if in a steep tunnel aimed toward the ground.

Suddenly her feet touched the ground and the vines in front of her parted. Rachel tumbled out into a small garden. When Aly reached down to help her up, Rachel gasped. "You're OK!"

"We all are." Rissa's voice came from beside her. Rachel turned to see all the girls. They looked fine except for the bits of leaves and twigs in their hair that added to their overall bedraggled condition. They were dirty, tattered and scratched. Every single one of them had the nastiest matted hair Rachel had ever seen. But seeing that they were OK, Rachel nearly cried with relief.

"What happened?" she asked.

"Well," Aly said, "they wouldn't leave the Wellspring unprotected, but I realized they didn't need to. We didn't need them to go away and let anyone through. We just needed them to let *us* through." She grinned. "Once I sent them a picture of us slipping through the vines, they let us in." Aly gestured toward the clearing. "Rachel, this is the garden from my dream. The one I'm going to put in the mural in my room."

"Then that's the Wellspring." Rachel pointed to the center of the large clearing. A tall fountain stretched well above the girls' heads. It was surrounded by a huge stone pool. The girls walked toward it slowly, mouths open as they stared. Around the outside of the fountain's pool was an ankle-high stone wall, each rock fitting almost seamlessly against the next.

In the midst of the dry pool, six statues stood frozen, dancing around the Wellspring's center. They were young girls in long gowns, hand raised to the sky and faces filled with joy.

"That looks like me," Rissa said, pointing at one figure with short choppy hair. "And look, the little one looks like you, Shaylee! I think these statues are us. How could they be us?"

"Magic?" Marisol said, shrugging. "But look at the top of the fountain." She pointed. At the center of the fountain pool was a tall pile of stones. Each stone was cut in a perfect rectangle. The pile of stones reached high into the air like a model of a craggy mountain. At the very top, a winged unicorn seemed to be bursting from the stone. All around him, they could see solid sprays of water, frozen into an eerie ice sculpture.

"How can that be ice? It's not cold in here," Rissa asked, wonder filling her voice.

"It *is* ice," Marisol answered. "I can feel it from here." The others turned and looked at her, puzzled. She grinned at her friends and shrugged. "I think it's just part of my weird water magic."

Kaida frowned. "So we need ... a hair dryer? Something to melt the ice?"

Rachel stepped into the pool and walked closer to the center. As she passed one of the stone dancers, she saw something shimmering in the air. She stepped closer and realized she was looking at spider webs. They hung in the air like a lace curtain wall surrounding the fountain's center but seemingly attached to nothing.

"What do you see?" Aly asked, stepping over the low wall to follow her sister.

Rachel didn't answer, but reached out her hand. At the point where her finger touched the web, the thin strands burst into sparkles and dropped away. Immediately, six small spiders rushed to the spot and began spinning impossibly fast. In barely a second, the web was repaired.

"I saw a drop!" Marisol yelled. "A drop of the ice melted—I saw it fall!"

Aly had reached Rachel's side in time to see the spiders weave their repair. "This web must have something to do with the Wellspring's freeze."

"Then let's tear it down!" Kaida said. She turned and looked at the ground around her, then snatched up a long thick stick and stepped into the pool. Rissa grabbed another sturdy stick and followed Kaida. Marisol and Shaylee trailed along behind. Marisol's attention was still on the sparkling ice.

"I don't know ... ," Rachel said. Something about the spiders felt wrong to her—*really* wrong. Then, as Kaida and Rissa stomped across the pool, the spiders dropped from the repaired web and fell at Rachel's feet, making her jump back.

As soon as the spiders hit the smooth pool floor, they began to grow. Rachel and Aly scrambled backward immediately, plowing into Kaida and Rissa. The spiders grew to the size of hamsters, then cats and kept growing. Before long the girls were facing six wolf-sized spiders.

"Go away and we won't kill you," the largest spider warned, her voice silky.

"It can talk!" Kaida yelped.

"Why are you doing this?" Rachel asked as she continued to back away, her voice shaky. "Don't you know everything is going to die if we don't fix the Wellspring?"

"Not everything, Princess," the spider said. "The old tiresome things will pass away and make room for a new magic!" A chorus of spider voices echoed, "A new magic!"

"You mean dark magic," Rachel said.

"Interesting magic," the spider replied. "You may find you enjoy it."

"Enjoy seeing our new friends die?" Shaylee said.

"Enjoy being trapped here forever with you guys?" Rissa added. "You must be crazy as well as creepy."

The spiders turned toward Rissa and hissed, but the leader held up a hairy leg. "If you leave us alone, we will open the portal for you. As soon as our magic wins, we will send you home."

"Oh, yeah," Rissa snorted. "I'm totally sure you wouldn't lie to us."

The spiders chuckled. "The alternative is that we kill you and eat you. Your magic will help us make the transition to 'dark magic,' as you call it, quicker."

"I really don't want to be eaten by a spider," Shaylee whimpered, backing away.

Throughout the conversation, the girls had been backing slowly out of the fountain pool ... and the spiders had followed them.

"Why didn't the Guarded Forest keep you out of here?" Aly said. "How did you get past the protective magic?"

"We were tiny spiders," the leader said, laughing again. "Why would the trees or the guardians notice such tiny sparks of magic?"

"That's what I thought," Aly said quietly and she closed her eyes.

Rachel grinned, realizing what Aly had in mind. "Of course, you're not so tiny anymore—you're probably pretty hard to miss now."

The lead spider shrieked. "Stop the Earth Princess!" The spiders surged toward Aly, but Kaida and Rissa jumped in front of the quiet girl and slapped at the spider's hairy legs with their sticks. The spiders reared up and used their long front legs to sweep Kaida and Rissa aside.

Rachel jumped onto the back of the lead spider and began hammering at its head with one fist. "Leave my sister alone!" The spider bucked and shook to throw the girl off, but Rachel hung on tightly.

In the battle to protect Aly, neither the spiders nor the girls noticed the vine walls around the clearing unraveling. Soon thick vines raced across the ground toward the group. Then, just as two spiders converged to grab Aly, the vines whipped around the spiders' legs. The spiders slashed at the vines with their fangs, slicing away some, but new vines grabbed at them.

Shaylee and Marisol pulled Aly away from the fight and back toward the forest edge.

Rachel realized she was stuck on the back of the largest

spider. Though vines lashed at it, they couldn't completely subdue the huge thrashing creature and Rachel dared not jump off where she might be in reach of the spider's fangs. So she threw back her head and yelled as loudly as she could, "FLEET!"

With the vine walls unwoven, a clear passage lay between the clearing and the woods. With an answering roar, Fleet limped into the clearing, followed by Honeyglow. Though clearly exhausted already from the lack of Wellspring magic, the bears never hesitated. They charged the lead spider. Honeyglow grabbed Rachel's thick cloak in her teeth and pulled the girl from the spider's back at the same time that Fleet began hammering the evil creature with clawed paws. Rachel heard Fleet's voice, sounding thin in her head. "Restore the magic, now!"

"We have to restore the magic before the Guardians weaken any more," Rachel shouted. The girls dashed around the struggling spiders and ran across the Wellspring pool. Kaida and Rissa slashed at the magic webs, ripping them away easily with their thick sticks.

The spout of frozen water at the top of the Wellspring burst into motion. Marisol held out her hands and the water flew over the girl's heads to splash across the struggling spiders. The spiders screamed as the water struck them and, they immediately began to shrink.

Rachel spotted one scuttling toward the forest's edge. "They're getting away!"

"Not important," Fleet panted, collapsing to the ground. "The Wellspring."

The girls turned back to the fountain. No water gushed forth. "It's not fixed yet," Marisol moaned. "I feel the water; but it's trapped somehow."

"We need a plumber!" Kaida complained. "Or at least some kind of instructions."

The girls looked around the piled rock base of the fountain itself and Rissa suddenly yelled, "I think I found the instruction book." Strange symbols were carved into the biggest stone.

"Wish we knew what that said," Kaida complained. "Even instruction manuals can't be easy in this place!"

"I can read it," Rissa said with a grin. "Part of me sees it like gibberish, but I still can read it. Weird!"

"Must be part of your spellcraft power," Rachel asked. "Does it seem to be a spell?"

"I'm not sure. It says, *'Bring forth light. Bring forth water. Bring forth magic and restore.'*"

"Light?" Rachel said. "Fire's like light. Maybe you're supposed to make a fire, Kaida."

Kaida shook her head. "I think I know what I'm supposed to do. It came to me as Rissa was reading."

"Me, too," Marisol said.

The two girls joined hands and closed their eyes while the others watched anxiously. Suddenly light, as bright as a summer day, poured down into the clearing. As it struck the center of the Wellspring, the whole fountain began to glow. Then rain fell from the cloudless sky, splashing into the pool around their feet.

"Now we dance," Rissa shouted over the sound of

the falling rain. "We're supposed to dance in the spaces between the statues!"

The girls spread out, each taking up a spot between two statues ... filling in the spaces to make a solid ring around the Wellspring's center. "Say the words while we dance, Rissa," Shaylee said as she started her movements and the others followed.

"*Bring forth light,*" Rissa called as they girls stepped forward and spun.

"*Bring forth water.*" They stepped back and spun.

"*Bring forth magic and restore.*" They held their arms high in the air and spun faster and faster, feeling giddy with sudden joy.

At that moment, the rain and glowing sunlight stopped, and instead, water burst forth from the fountain, spouting high in the air. As it fell back into the stone pool, they could see it wasn't ordinary water. It glowed silver, like moonlight in a shadowy clearing. As each drop struck the pool, the light separated from the water and poured out over the low stone wall and flowed across the clearing.

When the light touched each of the girls, they changed. Rachel looked down, laughing, to see her ragged filthy shred of a gown restored to its richly ornamented purple. Sleeves flowed down her arms like water, sheer and light as the finest silk. The fitted bodice was decorated with fine silver embroidery of bears and other animals. Rachel looked up at the other girls.

Shaylee's pink gown was shorter, only slightly below her knees, and everything about it looked light and airy.

Marisol wore a gown of deep royal blue with a bodice covered in sequins sewn to look like fish scales. Her hair was braided with strings of pearls. Kaida's gown was burnished gold, matching her eyes and making her coffee-colored skin glow. Rissa's gown was fiery red and embroidered all over with the same strange alphabet as the words carved into the fountain.

Then Rachel looked at her sister. Aly now wore a deep emerald gown embroidered with glistening ivy that trailed down her arms. Aly pointed toward the edge of the woods. "Look!" she cried.

The vines that had formed the walls to the clearing and taken part in the battle against the spiders had reformed into animal topiaries filled with flowers. Nothing stood between the clearing and the forest. The rest of the Guardians lumbered into the clearing and bowed toward the girls. They looked even bigger and stronger than ever

Laughing, the girls waded out of the fountain's pool to meet them. As soon as the girls stepped into the clearing, the magic water fell away from their clothes and they were dry. "Cool trick," Rissa said. "I wish I could do that in my shower!"

Rachel ran to Fleet and threw her arms as far around his thick neck as she could reach. "I'm so glad you're okay!"

Fleet's voice sounded in her head. "I always knew we would be." He gently pulled away from Rachel and took his place with the other Guardians. Then the bears rose up onto their hind legs and stretched their front paws high, and as they did, they changed. Their thick fur grew transparent, then dissolved altogether to reveal that they were young people with tousled golden hair. They wore long, brown, close-fitting tunics and leggings.

Fleet looked only a few years older than Rachel, though he was nearly a foot taller. He stepped forward and bowed again. "You have met your task," Fleet said in a clear voice. "Thank you, Princesses."

"You're not a bear!" Rachel blurted out. Instantly she felt silly for saying something so obvious and a little embarrassed about the hug.

"I am a Guardian. I take whatever form is needed," he said, smiling. "Part of the magic of the Guarded Forest is that few things are completely as they seem. When the magic was drained, we could no longer change. You have given all of us our forms back. Thank you."

"I wondered why it seemed like bears could talk to Rachel, and river dragons couldn't really talk to me at all," Marisol said. "I don't suppose my dragon friend is really a cute guy in disguise?"

"No," Fleet said, smiling slightly. "But I expect he is a better swimmer than any 'cute guy.'"

"But the spiders all talked," Rachel said.

"They were Spellmasters who had taken the form of spiders," Fleet explained.

"Spellmasters?" Rissa echoed. "But wouldn't I be their Princess since I'm Princess Spells-a-lot."

"You can only lead those who will follow."

"That's really deep," Shaylee said, pulling on Rissa's arm. "But can we just go home now?"

"You have restored the magic," Fleet said. "You can come and go as you like."

"Come and go as we like?" Rachel repeated as she heard the other girls gasp.

"We can come back?" Rissa asked.

Fleet nodded. "Use the keys. They will always open the door from your world to ours."

"I hate to be a party pooper," Kaida said. "But once we get home, our parents aren't going to let us out of their sight for years. We've been gone for days, and now we're going home in weird clothes with a crazy explanation for where we've been and how we're dressed. Can you say 'grounded for life'?"

Fleet laughed. "You may return home to the place and the moment you left, and you may wear whatever clothes you like."

"We can get our regular clothes back?" Rachel asked.

"And no one will even know we left?" Kaida added.

"You are Princesses. Simply wish it," Then Fleet smiled at Rachel. "Though I think your gown suits you well."

Rachel blushed at the compliment. But she closed her eyes and pictured her comfy jeans and all the clothes that made her feel totally normal. When she opened her eyes again, she grinned. She and the other girls were dressed in their usual clothes—even Rissa's hair was back to its crazy colors. Now, however, Rachel laughed out loud at how *normal* rainbow hair could look after everything else they'd seen on their adventure.

"Oh, no!" Shaylee gasped. She quickly pushed up her

pant leg and then smiled. The leather thong with the sunrise-colored bead was still on her ankle. "I didn't want to lose that."

"You need not lose anything," Fleet said. "This is your home now, too. Come and go as you like. You will always be our Princesses."

Shaylee narrowed her eyes. "If we come back, will we have more scary adventures?"

Fleet shrugged. "I can't see the future."

"I hope we come back," Kaida said.

Shaylee pointed at her friend. "No more gross stuff. I hate being dirty and wet and cold and hungry."

Rachel smiled. She was glad they'd be able to come back, but she thought she might be ready for some normal life again. "How do we get home now?"

"Join hands and picture where you want to be," Fleet said. "Your magic will open the door." He turned to Rachel and touched her hand. "I hope you will come again, Princess of the Guardians."

"I will," Rachel said. "Maybe not right away—but I will"

Her friends were already holding hands when Rachel walked over to join them. She clasped hands with Aly and Rissa. They all closed their eyes and pictured their familiar clubhouse in their minds.

The grassy circle in front of them changed to slightly worn gray carpet, and the girls were standing beside the table, hands clasped.

"That was the coolest thing ever!" Rissa breathed.

"Are we going back?" Aly asked.

"Not today," Shaylee said firmly.

"Not today," Kaida agreed "but someday."

"Someday soon," Marisol added. "I still would like to meet the mermaids."

The girls walked over to the table where their magical keys lay scattered, no longer stuck together or to the wood. Each girl picked up her key, the images of which were now both more meaningful and more mysterious.

"I'm glad there's a dragon on mine," Marisol said. "It will remind me of my new friends."

"So will mine," Rachel folded her hand over the image of the bear.

"Hey, we never saw the creature on my key except for that statue at the top of the Wellspring," Kaida said, holding out her triangle. "I hope it's real. Flying unicorns would be so cool."

Shaylee shivered, "I'm in no hurry. I'm not that wild about heights."

Rachel ran her thumb gently over the bear on her key. "You know, we never found out where these keys came from. I can't really picture a post office nestled in the Guarded Forest."

"Maybe you can ask Fleet the next time we go," Rissa said. "I'm sure you want to see *Fleet* again!"

Rachel blushed and gave Rissa a gentle push. Rissa giggled. "Well, you've gotta admit—our summer just got a lot more interesting!"

The girls laughed and hugged before heading for the clubhouse door and home.

What kind of Creative Girl are you?

Take our five-minute quiz at
CreativeGirlsClub.com to find out!

Every girl is creative in her own special way.

The six girls in this book discover this truth as they experience exciting adventures and solve some very tough mysteries. Even though they're all great friends, they are also very different from one another. And each one has a very special talent to contribute to the their club.

After you read this thrilling story, visit our web site at CreativeGirlsClub.com to find out more about your own special creative interests. Just take our short quiz at the Web site to learn about your greatest creative passion. Plus, we'll tell you which of the six Creative Girls Club girls is the most like you creatively!

Happy reading,

Laura Scott

Laura Scott, editor

**For more information about this
Creative Girls Club Adventure Book, go to**

CreativeGirlsClub.com

- Take our short quiz to discover your greatest creative interest.

- Learn about the Creative Girls Club craft kit series, in which Club members get two exciting new craft kits every six weeks.

- Read messages and ideas from Creative Girls Club members from all over the country.

This Creative Girls Adventure Book is published by DRG, 306 E. Parr Road, Berne, IN 46711. For more information about us and our Creative Girls Club craft kit series, call toll-free, (877) 226-5391.